Who's Next?

"Alton!" Meggie finally screamed so abruptly that the name loosed her throat, straightened out all the crooked words and now she screamed that she had found Alton . . . between screaming hiccups . . . dead.

"Alton? Who's Alton?" her mother asked as she crawled out of bed to call the law.

"You don't mean the Alton Gillespie you told me about yesterday?"

Meggie nodded.

First Billy Watson. Now Alton Gillespie. Why?

Lightning zipped through Meggie's throbbing head.

point

JOURNEY

Joyce Carol Thomas

SCHOLASTIC INC.
New York Toronto London Auckland Sydney

I thank Mitch Douglas for his superior agenting and excellent advice.

I thank Jean Feiwel for continuing to ask the right editorial questions.

I thank my family.

I thank the spirit.

jct

ISBN 0-590-40628-0

12 11 10 9 8 7 6 5 4 3 2 1   2   0 1 2 3 4 5/9

Printed in the U.S.A.   01

And there shall be no night there;
and they need no candle,
neither light nor the sun;
for the Lord God giveth them light:
and they shall reign forever and ever.
—Revelation 22:5

Once upon a time
Sages believed the tarantula's bite
Created the most compelling urges
Those bitten would not be still or
keep quiet
They spoke in and out of turn in
spite of themselves

Prologue

In the deep blue lap of night Meggie Alexander, a nutmeg-colored infant with a birthmark in the middle of her forehead, lay in her cradle trying to braid the moonbeams trailing through her window, but the misty light kept slipping through her fingers.

Then one evening when the frost on the fig tree looked like stardust, a dappled brown tarantula with a lightning stripe across her back crawled into the dimples of Meggie's hand and tickled her.

Meggie giggled.

The tarantula, taking this giggle as a welcome sign, sighed a long string of silk and started weaving picture stories.

Although tarantulas have not been known to spin webs and hang from cradles and doorways, Meggie's tarantula was different. She spun gossamer tales that thrilled the baby and relaxed her at the same time.

When the child's eyelids drooped heavily, the spider knew her bedtime stories had worked their soothing magic on each shimmering spoke of the round, round web.

The pleased spider stopped weaving in the middle of a spoke and knelt down on her eight legs so she could admire the way the jasper stars twinkled against Meggie's nutbrown skin, bathing her face in blue shadows.

Meggie was a change-of-life baby.

Her mother, Memory Alexander, had thought her child-bearing days had passed her by. She was fast approaching fifty when the baby's blood first whispered in her ear and her husband, Michael Leon Alexander, was on his way to fifty.

"Old people's children come here looking wrinkled and ugly," Midnight Alexander warned from the rocking chair in her room, richly smelling of fresh paint, liniment and vitamins.

"I hear you, Mama," Michael Alexander had said, standing on a stepladder busily painting one half of his mother's room iris-lavender.

In the corner, a corncrake Midnight had insisted on bringing from Oklahoma ruffled his short wings and hollered in a cage, wanting to be out slipping through reeds around some muddy lake.

"I can't believe you're going to put death and birth in the same chamber," Midnight Alexander had complained to the pregnant Memory. "Something all broke down next to something new. I'm like some old worn-out car. Fix one thing, something else breaks. Tamed the arthritis, now diabetes is bucking. I tell you you'd better free my corncrake and carry me on to the old folks' home today, my bags are packed."

"We couldn't bear that," said Memory, pausing, her brush dripping iris-blue in tiny specks on the golden oak floor.

"Anyway, just last year at ninety you were still going out to the pasture feeding the cows," said Michael.

2

"That's the problem," Midnight reflected. "I should have stayed there last winter and kept my mouth shut. No, I had to go tell you about taking the axe and breaking the ice so the cattle could drink. Next thing I know I'm spirited from Oklahoma to California, sitting up here listening to my bones talk back to me. I never heard them then when I was taking care of my own business on my own farm. Old people should work as long as they can. All these years I've been waiting for a grandchild from you two and just when I've resigned myself to not having one, since you're both too old and Memory ready to go through the change, you come up pregnant. I repeat, old folks' babies come here looking wrinkled and ugly!"

But Meggie didn't come here looking wrinkled and ugly. She came here nutmeg-colored, smooth-cheeked, dimpled with a small birthmark in the middle of her forehead.

She was coming in as Grandma Alexander was going out. Grandma Alexander took one look at her brand-new grandchild and said, "Well, sir, I've been waiting ninety years for this.

"Carry on," she whispered just before she closed her midnight eyes, gave up the ghost and became pure spirit.

Meggie was born screaming into the light that November morning; her grandma, on her way to heaven, stopped to gather morning glories in a garden of stars and did not yen for earthly candles as she gathered the flowers to her breath. Time, watching her, struck twelve bells that fateful evening. Midnight passed between today and tomorrow.

3

"Carry on."

And carry on they did as though it was a chant threading through their lives, "carry on."

Memory, in age two generations removed from Meggie, had a storehouse of wisdom saved up to pass along to her daughter.

The gray-haired Memory, the silver-haired Michael walked, exercised and continued to work — Memory as a junior high school teacher, Michael as a captain in the medical corps of the army. Continued to work to keep old age, heart attacks, rheumatism, and high blood at bay and to keep their minds alert.

"Snow on the chimney; fire in the oven. Feel so good I just might live to be one hundred," Captain Michael Alexander acknowledged his snow-white hair and flexed his muscles as he heated up Meggie's formula.

"Me too," said Memory, rocking the infant and thinking, here's all the children we ever wanted rolled up into one and judging from how passionately Meggie hollered for life, it would take two centuries worth of wisdom to raise her.

Another frosty night so cold and clear the stars looked like chips of ice in the midnight sky, the midnight spider returned to the nursery. Hanging from her loop of silk she touched the crinkled wisps of Meggie's curls.

And the black locks sprang back as they were.

"Wish my brown hair would bounce like that," whispered the tarantula.

But it was Meggie's giggle that inspired the best picture stories.

From the living room, party sounds drifted into the nursery.

"New house. New baby. All cause for celebration!" cheered Meggie's parents to the happy guests.

The sounds of crystal glasses breaking in the blazing fireplace echoed down the hallway.

"Hear that? That Captain daddy of yours is home on leave and he'll be leading People in here any minute to admire your sparkling eyes," said the spider to the baby and she scampered surreptitiously to the linen closet.

There the tarantula worked, standing up on her eight legs, mixing her poison, and scooting her many eyes around in her head.

When the tarantula got finished fixing her poison, she sat down and spun her silk like a lady, sewing and humming.

Finally the celebration wound down.

"See you at church on Sunday," somebody hollered in parting.

"Where'd you find that baby? She's absolutely too stunning for this world and with that mark in the middle of her mind."

"Middle of her forehead," said Meggie's mother.

"That's what I said. Middle of her mind," claimed the old visitor, once the bosom buddy of the recently departed Midnight Alexander, leaning on her crooked cane.

"Sure some ancient fairy didn't leave her on your doorstep?"

A laugh from the other departing guests.

The slam of a car door.

The old visitor was spending the night on the couch.

She asked, "Where do you keep the bed sheets?"

The spider stopped weaving and listened for the

answer, her heart dropping down to her eight knees.

Her one worry was discovery of her residence on the top shelf.

"In the middle drawer in the linen closet," answered Michael Alexander.

The woman with the crooked cane did not stretch arms up to reach the high cedar shelf where the spider worked.

The spider, undisturbed, finished weaving her silk and looked around for a tasty mosquito or a tempting fly.

It was dinnertime and she was hungry.

After she ate two biting flies and one fat moth, she waited for the parents and guest to go to bed, longing to see Meggie.

In the meantime, the spider took a short nap herself, sleeping with three of her eight eyes open.

Finally when the embers flickered in the freestone fireplace and the only sound was the November rain falling in fat sparkles against the windowpane, the spider pulling her ball of silk behind her, threaded her way into the nursery.

Because she had no bones, she was as lithe as a feather.

She threw a line of silk like a lasso and shimmying up it, heisted herself over the cradle railing and began spinning a new web with the ease of a native spider.

Meggie giggled.

Too loud.

The spider stopped her calligraphy.

And Meggie stopped giggling.

Somebody stirred.

And then the sound of footsteps.

Uh oh.

At the slightest warning, a cough from the grown people's room or a slipper slapping across the floor, the spider untangled herself from the cradle slat and flowed down like brown-legged river water. There on the floor she buried herself in the carpet, becoming inconspicuous, looking only like a shadow or some innocent stain.

The orange-brown color of the rug reminded the tarantula of the copper leaves on the ground up in Eucalyptus Forest where she once danced in the wild.

The two of them were coming, Michael and Memory Alexander, to check the baby for wetness or hunger or illness.

"Was that a cry or a laugh?" Memory asked.

"Sounded like a laugh to me," said Michael.

"What could she be laughing about? Anyway, she's too little to laugh, she's only old enough to smile."

Because they did not expect to see anything like it, when the parents looked into the cradle at Meggie, they did not notice the intricate almost invisible web.

"Oh, she's all right," they cooed.

Memory took off Meggie's wet diaper.

"Hand me the powder, Michael," she said.

When Michael reached into the pocket, there was only air.

"No more left," he answered.

"Impossible," said Memory. "That pack's supposed to have six cans of talcum!"

"See for yourself," said Michael, taking over to pin the baby's diaper on Meggie, not clumsy as the spider

7

would have expected since they don't teach diaper skills in the army.

"Imagine that! Shortchanging us!" complained Memory. "Why, that corner store merchant's as crafty as a spider and as crooked as its web!"

The listening tarantula took the insult personally.

And the devil got into the tarantula.

Before the mama followed the daddy back down the hallway, the spider somersaulted down her silk string to the floor beside the nearsighted Memory, knowing full well the woman couldn't see her.

"Old lizard lady!" the spider hissed.

Memory looked down but she didn't see anything.

It was all the tarantula could do to keep her fangs from sinking into the woman's skinny toothpick ankles.

"A walleyed heifer!" pouted the spider.

When the house had quieted down again, and she could hear all the people snoring so hard they rattled the windows, the spider talked to Meggie about Memory's offensive remark.

While she chattered, with her spider dancing mouth, she wove a web from one side of the cradle to the other, generous with her silk. A spider speaking in tongues.

"People're always saying things like 'spiteful as a spider.' Yes, we have been called creepy, crooked, crafty and cold.

"And folks don't discriminate.

"They throw us all in the same spider bag, from my wolf spider cousins, to the black widow clan, and the labyrinth branch, even the sack spiders and the brown widows and red widows get mashed together in the name-calling.

8

"No respect, even though we protect the earth from crop-eating locusts and disease-carrying mosquitoes.

"I don't mean to brag, but I've been present at all the cataclysmic events in this here old world. Witnessed earthquakes, tornadoes, whirlwinds and typhoons. 'Course I put down my spinning wheel and laid low, what do you think?

"I get so sick and tired of common folk trying to put their nobody feet on my queenly head. Me? I was present in the first world. Furthermore," the spider boasted, squinting her crooked eyes, "I come from a loooong line of royalty and famous people. Millions of years ago I saw the first rainbow. I ruled as the Egyptian historical arachnid. Cleopatra's last confidante. I'm somebody."

The sun was rising, the night over, and through the nursery window colors gathered.

The spider then finished her patterned story, and while Meggie giggled at the odd ways the lines curved and leaped just over her bed, the spider sucked in her waist, climbed up her silk hose of a dragline and looked out the window at the sky.

"Look a yonder! A colored bridge to heaven!" the spider exclaimed. "A rainbow. Now, there's a pleasing pattern!"

And Meggie wanted to braid the watercolors into a shawl for her shoulders, a quilt for her cradle.

The tarantula crawled down out of the bed just as the mama rounded the corner shaking a warm baby bottle in her hand.

Mornings alone and quiet in the closet the spider measured her worth, she was of benefit in general to the earth, but also of benefit in particular to this house. More than once she had heard Memory Alexander remark that the house stayed free of flies and mice, "And not a cat around."

Memory Alexander had been repeating this observation for over a month. "House free of flies and mice and not a cat around."

It was over a month ago, the day after Meggie's grandmother took herself on up to grandma heaven, that the tarantula had discovered Meggie's house.

Meggie asked, "How?"

"The discovery went like this," said the tarantula.

"I had me a cousin, a wonderful black widow woman named Johanna Hopkins. After we'd come down from Eucalyptus Forest carrying our poisons and our silks, I said to the black widow that I had reserved a place to stay.

" 'Reservations?' asked the black widow.

"Then an argument broke out over who would stay in your house, Meggie.

" 'I think I should be the one,' said the black widow, her natural selfish self-centeredness loomed.

" 'No,' I said, 'because in the process of making my reservations I already investigated.'

" 'Investigated'? asked Johanna, who could be all venom and mouth. Mouth, Lord that widow could talk.

" 'Yes, ma'am. And I already determined the carpet's the color of a tarantula spider,' " I said most proudly.

"The black widow, putting her hands on her spider hips, rejoined, 'I only believe what I see and none of what I hear; you've got to show me!' and she climbed the wall of the house herself and took one look in the window and wholeheartedly agreed.

When she saw the rug, she said, 'Well, shut my mouth!' and she left quicker than a jumping spider rumored to jump twenty times the length of its body.

"The last thing I saw of my cousin Johanna she was moving through the high grass, heading for higher ground, reeling in her loneliness, in search of a black widow mansion in Eucalyptus Forest under some fallen tree trunk where she'd feel right at home."

"The end," said the web.

Next time the tarantula visited Meggie in the nursery was a stormier night. The wind had its back up and sounded like a train traveling, clickety-clack, rak-a-tak-tak over the house.

The spider wound down out of the closet on her silk rope and ambled along the wall and into the nursery.

Thunder echoed and stomped in giant boots across the sky.

Thin steel-threaded winds choo-chooed at the windows and screeched in a language that only babies and spiders understand.

The tarantula lifted one of her hairy eight legs and tickled the baby in her dimple.

Meggie woke up and giggled.

The tarantula said all spidery-voiced, "I don't know why grown folks act so scared of spiders. They ought to take a lesson from babies. Why, in the entire state of California have you ever heard of a baby killed by a spider? 'Course not! We understand each other. But grown folks getting pinched by me and my cousins don't smell a bit like sweet anise and talcum powder."

The spider shrugged. "They smell like fear."

11

"Can't stand fear, it makes me want to bite somebody," said the spider with humor.

"Fear, fear, fear," giggled the baby in spider language, not quite understanding the emotion, having never experienced it.

"Why, I'd make a perfect baby-sitter," continued the spider, and she began to weave another allegorical web.

"Better'n a guard dog," she added.

"Guard dog," mimicked Meggie.

The spider crossed her many legs. "Imagine somebody coming into the nursery with me in here. I'd only have to hunch my hairy back and nod and they'd scram!"

Then the storm rubbed the electrical lines against the tall old oak trees lining the street and blew out all the power, so even the night-light didn't glow enough for Meggie to see the web story the spider had written. Clouds had strangled the pumpkin moon, so no light from that source either.

When the circling clouds loosed their hold on the winter night, and the sun rose, the spider wanted to stay longer in the warm and fragrant bed.

But footsteps swished and she bade Meggie goodbye and scampered down and on past the slippered feet of the sleepy-eyed Memory and dashed up the ajar closet door and onto the rosebed of cotton sheets.

There she kicked her eight legs against the rough closet wall doing a hot spider dance.

The spider heard the mother say, "Gicchy, gicchy goo," to Meggie, then add, "My precious, how bright your eyes are, just like you've seen a little magic."

"Of course," murmured the spider under her breath, doing an easy eight-step, "I'm the magic."

Her dancing done, the spider got into her most creative mood. She began a large project, her most ambitious to date.

An intricate web. Its breadth so vast it would, when finished, cover the entire top shelf.

The tarantula got so involved she took a holiday from Meggie.

And every day Meggie boo-hooed and called unceasingly for the spider until her voice grew hoarse.

"The baby's got the croup," the tarantula heard Memory Alexander say to her husband.

"Croup, my eye!" hooted the spider, "she's pining for me."

Finally after the spider had finished crocheting her best web she went back to the crib for a visit.

And just in time. Meggie was beginning to become less fluent in the spider language and could say words like "mama," "daddy," "bottle," and "water."

Meggie's hair was even bouncier and thick enough to hold in place for fat braids. About the head she looked like a doll-sized version of her mama.

"You've grown, honey," sighed the spider, admiring the three braids like a triple-threaded rhythm on each side of Meggie's head.

"And so have your webs," Meggie answered touching the sticky silk perfection.

When Meggie smiled, not giggled, at the silk pattern, the spider could see bumps where teeth would emerge.

This depressed the tarantula, but she tried not to let it show. Meggie's innocence, the spider knew, could not last. The dimples in her hands were not as snuggly deep. She had grown an inch.

"Why, keep growing like this, you're gonna be as straggly as your mama. An Amazon girl."

"Tell me a story," Meggie cooed.

And the spider wove the story of her black widow cousin, Johanna Hopkins, who vowed to set a record by marrying the most husbands in the territory, the ancient black widow game of husband trapping.

"You've heard of one-upmanship? She practiced one-upwidowship. Why, the woman had seven husbands in one month!"

"Am I a People or a spider?" asked Meggie, intrigued by the black widow's shenanigans.

The tarantula waited a long time before responding; it was the hardest question she had ever answered. "You're a People," said the spider.

The baby caught her breath sharply as if she wanted to turn her sigh to silk and couldn't.

Resigned to her lot in life, Meggie fell into a baby-soft sleep. The spider squatted in the story web listening to the rhythm of Meggie's breath blowing against the web and smelling the licorice aroma of sweet anise.

The tarantula became mesmerized by the whisper of wind which was Meggie's breath, the way it pushed the crocheted web of Johanna's seven husbands back and forth, back and forth.

Hypnotized.

Next thing the spider knew, Memory Alexander stepped into the nursery and froze at the sight of the poisonous spider hovering over her innocent child.

The light ebbed pale in there.

But the shadow of movement disturbed the spider, bringing her out of her reverie.

Now the tarantula was fully awake.

She felt what was coming right down her boneless spine.

She stayed very still as the nearsighted mother inched closer to make sure she wasn't mistaken. . . .

Certain now about the hairy creature, Memory Alexander hollered, the force of her lungs untangled the intricate web and seven husbands fell like gossamer wings over Meggie's face.

"Tarantula, my spider," Meggie, now awake, cried in their language, frightened for the first time in her life, not for herself but for her friend, the storytelling spider woman.

Memory Alexander snatched her baby from under the silken veil and for a brief moment clutched Meggie close to her like a sack of whole wheat flour with eyes.

Abruptly she sat the baby down on the floor and found her weapon. A prior month's *Life* magazine.

Smash.

"You can run, Mrs. Spider, but you just can't hide," Memory Alexander chanted as she lifted the *Life* magazine to issue out Death.

Meggie, sensing how precious little time was left, spoke to the spider in a singsong voice, like a harp was caught in her throat, "So much I wanted to ask you, Mrs. Spider, how to weave the wind into scarlet ribbons. . . ."

The spider, hearing Meggie, hunkered down dodging the magazine.

Smash.

Meggie continued, "I want to borrow the water-color-blue from the rainbow to dye my yarn for the colored shawl."

"Run on, but you cannot hide," the mother repeated.

"I want to leave a spell in the threads purple as amethyst in autumn."

Smash.

"Run on, but you cannot hide," the mother repeated.

"How many strings would it take, I wonder?" asked Meggie in that music voice.

The tarantula moaned, her time running out, answered, "Five or six." Thinking of all the lessons she had meant to teach the child she managed to respond, "Meggie, get yourself a guitar, a loom of strings, an audible loom. Meggie, be a queue-jumping, jaywalking woman.

"Shimmer when you jump, glitter when you walk."

The message echoed in Meggie's ear.

Smash.

"You can. . . ."

From way off Meggie could hear the spider holler, "But whatever you do, Meggie, let nothing, nobody, separate you from the light."

The mama couldn't understand any of this.

Smash.

"Run but. . . ."

Finally the spider, in a beaten voice, said, "They say babies develop amnesia. . . ."

"You just can't . . ." continued the mother.

Smash.

"Hide."

"But I know better," sighed the spider.

The spider's last words were these, "When Meggie's" — *smash* — "searching for the blue-peace shawl, reaching to braid the light" — *smash* — "she's thinking of me."

One

In the coming sunrise every wildflower flourishing in ditches and unkempt places, every blade of thirsty grass drinking dew before day, every web shimmering on the straggly backyard fences and every sigh of dusty wind seemed to be waiting for Meggie to wake up.

No voices in the gathering waiting spoke at first; sound seemed content to be one with the resilient wildflowers, part of the landscape.

Finally a solitary voice broke open and started to speak one, two, three words, like a too-early rain, starting to fall, then stopping halfway down from the sky. The voice was gone. Something was trapped here.

"Get up, Meggie!" the male voice spoke, then was silenced.

Fifteen-year-old Meggie, sound asleep, twisted and turned, balled up in the bed like the outline of a question mark.

Then some compassionate archangel dressed in white gauze with a crown of morning glories on her snow-white head whispered, "All our days are numbered, Meggie." And the angel sat down and gently turned her spinning wheel.

In her dream Meggie mounted a silver sky, climbing the stars stepping up one to the other, skipping up a hill of stars that glowed like bright crystal stepping stones lighting her way to heaven.

Then the archangel's spinning wheel turned into a glistening mahogany guitar and she bent her silver head over the strings as she strummed.

The guitar's sweet twang interrupted Meggie's skipping rhythm and her feet hesitated.

The broken voice freed itself from the trap and abruptly Meggie's eyes flew open when she heard it, more startling than the guitar, repeat, "Get up, Meggie."

Now that her eyes were open, the male voice was gone. The stars had disappeared. Her feet were bedbound. No grandmotherly angel strummed a sacred guitar.

It had not been her father's voice. He was overseas on army assignment and would be gone at least a month.

The male voice in her dream had a chuckle in it same as Billy Watson's used to have.

Now she would only hear that voice in her dreams.

It was the morning of Billy Watson's funeral.

Billy Watson, her original gingerbread boy. Her chocolate Boy Wonder. Her buddy, her friend.

Meggie untangled herself from the purple quilt and the blue sheets, disturbing her mongrel dog, Redwood, so named because his coat was the color of redwood. Redwood yawned himself awake at the foot of her bed. And the sleepy-eyed Jehoshaphat, a fat tortoiseshell tomcat with golden eyes, nicknamed Fat for the last syllable in Jehoshaphat and because he was fat, uncurled himself from the curve of her elbow.

"Time to leave already," she said eyeing the clock next to the handsome portrait of her father in military uniform and her mother in schoolteacher dress.

"Redwood, you stay home with Jehoshaphat today, you hear?" Her mother had flown to the Panhellenic Council of the Sigma Gamma Rhos, AKA's and Delta sororities up in Oregon State and wouldn't be back until Sunday night.

Redwood whined, sad-eyed and droopy-eared, a little unhappy about obeying this order to guard the house when he wanted to be at Meggie's heels.

Time to leave this room of cotton textures and rainbow colors, Meggie thought.

No time to play her guitar while sitting in her concert chair, an avocado-green chair planted beneath the cotton curtains in cool colors scampering and running down her windows.

How her thumb ached for the mahogany guitar waiting mutely on the corner chair.

She got up and didn't take time to make her bed. She left the chenille pink bedspread tangled all up with the pale blue sheets and the purple crazy-patch quilt.

"Billy, Billy Watson," she said to her mirror as she pulled the comb through her thick hair. When the mirror didn't answer her, she stopped with the comb in midair, leaving the great curls to riot mournfully all over her head.

Thickly sighing she plodded to her closet and pushing aside the blue jeans and assorted sweaters and shirts she usually favored, she chose a checkered black skirt, a cotton black high-collared blouse and slipped into a pair of tight, rarely used, toe-pinching ebony patent-leather flats.

On her slow walk to Billy Watson's funeral, her mourning turned to rage. And with the storm of emotion came a terrible, lumbering energy. Her heavy steps carried her forward in spite of herself.

The cement sidewalks didn't help her mood either. She wanted earth under her feet and a jungle of trees for her canopy. She wanted to be up in Eucalyptus Forest with Billy Watson romping through the wild wheat meadows and listening to the corncrakes call back and forth, but Billy Watson who had had a sixteen-year-old's chuckle in his voice and who had lived three streets over on Hilgard had been found shot to death by some trigger-happy fool.

"Billy, Billy, Billy," a corncrake's song scampered in her ears as she found herself staring at the long black hearse squatting like a grotesque cockroach in front of the church.

The sound of Billy's name made her hand tremble on the doorknob to the sanctuary of Perfect Peace Baptist Church.

"Why? Why? Why?" she asked the wind.

Getting no answer, she turned the knob and entered.

The choir, robed in black, hummed some old mournful song.

The song sagged. "We Shall Overcome" sounded like we never shall. The key dragged. The words didn't believe themselves. They would not soar. Dried-up hope. Let down dignity into a drought-dry well.

Meggie stood watching the people packed in the church blur into a crowd of dark somber dresses and suits, and the sight of the casket wouldn't let her sit down. A scalding rage ran from the top of her head down to the bottom of her feet.

Every time she tried to sit the sight of that silver casket pulled her up and the sound of the corncrake calling Billy's name like a bell burst in her ears. She opened her mouth and couldn't close it. And the grief-ring in her voice made the mourners unbow their heavy heads.

She raved, "Why, more young folk than old're getting buried, and you're talking about 'Yea though I walk through the valley of the shadow of death. . .'? What are we going to do about this?" Meggie asked of each face raining grief. "We don't want to walk through the valley of the shadow of death. We want to run up the hillside in the sunshine of life."

Dennis Bell gave a coughing kind of laugh. Peel-headed Dennis, the son of the Battling Bells, sat shyly on the back bench, alone and detached from the funeral mourners. A strange teenager with a limp in his mind, Meggie thought. An old young man who always did the opposite of what good sense dictated. Something awkwardly lopsided in his lanky arms, his hanging shoulders.

"Got dropped on his head as an infant," Meggie's mother once explained with frustrated compassion.

"How?" Meggie had wondered.

"In one of those infernal battles that the Bells pitched. Crib shattered. Instead of crying Dennis was lying there on the floor, wet as a turtle, diaper hadn't been changed since the battle began early that morning. Dennis, just grinning up at us, his rescuers, like he was the king ant at a July Fourth picnic.

22

"Bells, drunk as skunks, had fought 'til they dropped, selfish, mindless of the child, cold and wet and helpless in that house of Scotch drinking and angry-at-the-world, sorry parents."

Remembering all that, Meggie turned and gave Dennis a sympathetic look that shut him up, that made him scoot down lower in his seat and sink his head deeper into the well between his shoulders.

At the front of the church Reverend Hawkins, all humped over, crouched on his knees in private conversation with the Lord, asking, "Dear God, what shall I tell these poor people?"

He got no answer from the Higher Power, but he did hear Meggie's cry. He couldn't get a prayer through, but Meggie's lament caught his ears. Slowly he pulled himself up off his aching knees.

"Church, some of us are not holding up so well," he explained to the congregation in sympathy for Meggie's sorrow.

"Daughter, you're just grieving," he said tired, tired of preaching so many funerals for the young. It was all a riddle. Cancer-riddled bodies. Bullet-riddled boys caught in the crossfire of gang fights. Drug-riddled OD's. Suicide riddles.

"Come on up, Miss Meggie, and look into the casket," Reverend Hawkins offered forlornly.

"I'm not," said Meggie. "I'm not looking in any more caskets at people my age. It's not natural. The only people supposed to be in the shadow are the old folks. I gotta think of some other way to live with my memory of Billy.

"Billy, Billy, Billy," she rasped, eyes brimming, transfixed by the sleet-gray casket.

23

Just then Reverend Marvella Franklin, sitting over in the Amen Corner so inconspicuous folks usually missed her until she opened her mouth, stood up.

"Evil walks and death stalks," she began hesitantly.

"Carry a light in your heart," she whispered.

The whirling words ran Meggie on out of the church house. And she roamed the streets, wearily searching for something she could not name. She went to the places she and Billy Watson had frequented and finally to the Bay Wolf Barbershop.

The barber standing on a small mountain of unswept hair just looked at her in an understanding way and nodded for her to take her seat on the stool where she usually waited for Billy.

Pretty soon the men seemed to forget the lonesome girl lingering so sorrowfully over in the corner beneath the calendar of dark movie stars and brown beauty queens.

They talked about Billy Watson.

Talk. She was sick of it.

But she listened anyway. Maybe some answer abided here, here at Bay Wolf Barbershop where Billy used to chuckle and join the men in careless and serious conversations.

All of a sudden Peter Watson, Billy's wino uncle, swayed in the doorway declaring, "They say Reverend Marvella Franklin got a prayer through."

The Right Reverend Lee Arthur Huntington, who had a habit of bringing up the controversial issue of 'can a woman preach?' shook off his barber's bib and rubbed his smooth freshly-shaved, fig-colored chin.

Eyes flashing with defiance, these words ran out

24

of Reverend Huntington's mouth and settled in the ear like a deep itch, "God called Paul he didn't call Paula! Called Elijah not Eliza. How many times do I have to tell the ministerial alliance to keep that woman out of the pulpit, don't be giving these women the power to preach?"

"You can't give what you ain't got," said Billy's wino uncle.

"What?" said the reverend.

"It's God's to give. Not man's. If He can make a axe talk, how come He can't make a woman preach?"

For Meggie, the answer to every question could be found in the results. Could she or couldn't she preach, this Reverend Marvella Franklin?

"Tell you one thing," said Billy Watson's uncle, sour wine making his speech slur, "when she opens her mouth up yonder on the Perfect Peace pulpit every devil in Berkeley takes off to beyond the city limits on the outskirts of town. Never mind that when Moses climbed the mountain the devil slid up there behind him. When Marvella Franklin climbs God's mountain she brandishes arrows, sticks and Godly stones. A snake ain't got chance one. She can look at you and read you. Why, she looked at me once and didn't a drop a liquor cross my lips for a month. What you got to remember in this old world is that the devil's alive and everybody ain't sanctified!"

"What's her text?" asked the mailman, taking Reverend Lee Arthur Huntington's place in the barber's chair.

"Choose," said the wino.

"Choose?"

"A one-worded text. Who ever heard. . . ?" Reverend Huntington didn't finish his sentence; disgusted he walked on out of the shop, down-turned fig mouth muttering something about the Bible saying let the women be quiet in the temple and shaking his head as he waddled, making a beeline to his own storefront church, to make sure the Missionary Group of women meeting that afternoon stayed ten feet from his pulpit as they studiously thumbed through the Bible in their course of interpreting it.

This "can-a-woman-preach?" conversation was reported to everybody who came to get a haircut. Needless to say Perfect Peace Baptist Church would be crowded come Sunday morning.

What did Marvella Franklin mean at the funeral when she said, "Carry a light in your heart," Meggie wondered and what does that and the oddly titled text, "Choose," have to do with Billy Watson?

Meggie was sitting in the front pew at Perfect Peace when Reverend Marvella Franklin brought the Sunday message.

"Evil walks and death stalks. Carry a light in your heart. If the light's in your heart can't anybody keep you from it. Can't anybody turn it out. Not even PG&E. If they cut off your electricity because you can't pay your bill you've still got the light. One day when I was feeling mighty low I went down to the river where nothing talked but the water and picked me up some stray sprigs of wood and built myself a fire where I could listen to God speak without interruption. One day you might not be by the water, you might not be by a place you can gather wood for an old-fashioned ordinary altar of fire, but if you carry a light in your heart this you can rely on, it will always be there. When you pray say these words,

'Most holy creator, God of the trees and everything that walks and swims and flies, stand by me!

" 'God of thunder, God of fire, lightning, water and cloud, deliver me in times of trouble, stand by me in times of joy, stand by me when the world begins to understand. Hear my plea, bend an ear to me, most mightiful, powerful, heavenly Creator stand by me.'

"And Church, that is my prayer. Now if I, stooped over as I was with agony, could straighten my back and choose, anybody can choose. My whole life was a river of pain. Couldn't anybody grieve and grumble more woe-be-gone than me. If you looked at me long my face would cloud up.

"First I tried to handle the hurt by myself. Woe to the person ever told me No. When I got through cursing them out and walking up and down their back with spikes, you could run a truck through where their feelings used to be. I was a dangerous woman! Sow the wind, reap the whirlwind.

"When I searched outside myself for consolation I fell in with all kind of false prophets, Bible-thumping bigots, wrongdoing rabbis, and money ministers. When I went to the so-called authorities for help I ran into jackleg politicians, wheeler-dealers, henchmen, finaglers and wire-pullers. It was about power. Wanted me to bow to them. Anybody knows me knows I don't bow down to nobody but God!

"God is the archconsoler. I say God is The Authority.

"And the joy you've got waiting, even the rainbow can't hold. . . . Can taste the blue skin of a blueberry and the inside-out purple beauty of a fig. I say you can hold music in your mouth and rest inside a note."

She broke out into one of those low husky shouts, her feet doing a sanctified dance, while the church members' voices popped up here and there waving her on, saying, "Amen."

"Now somebody might leave here thinking I don't like preachers. . . ." Her voice dipped, "I didn't say that. But not everybody up in the pulpit is anointed. You want to know why this woman's preaching? When the only power I ever respected called, I answered. Yes, I was *called* to preach! I know you've been talking about can a woman preach?

"Some of you even saying now if a woman can preach next thing they'll be claiming is God's a woman."

Now she declared so quietly some church members involuntarily scooted forward in their pews, *"God can be whatever God wants to be!"*

She went on and tied the sermon together, talking about choosing, then she ended it with these resounding words falling quiet as small sprinklings of nutmeg whispering into a bowl of whipping cream:

"Choose to live.

"Death dealing is the devil's duty.

"The devil's still swishing his long reptilian tail, hooding his ruby snake eyes, walking up and down seeing who he can devour, strewing banana peels on the steep path of life trying to see who he can trick into slipping. Be aware!

"Carry a light in your heart. Some of you're already shining like neon. Don't even need batteries; you've got everything you require to keep the light going. And God makes no mistakes.

"Choose.

"Carry a light in your heart and live!"

Meggie wondered, what's all this got to do with what happened to her Billy Watson, he couldn't have chosen to die, Billy with that chuckle in his voice.

Carry a light in your heart, the reverend woman had said; what on heaven and earth did she mean?

Two

The sunlight glittered on teenagers of all variety and colors and shapes that decorated the stucco-dotted campus at Berkeley High on Monday morning.

Redheaded skinny ones sprawled near the acacia bushes by the music department. Fat as butterball ones ate Snickers and Bit O'Honey candy bars, joyously littering the grounds with the wrappers, enough of the sticky sweetness glued to the waxy paper to draw armies of grateful ants.

Muscular jocks, black as molasses, white as vanilla, dribbled basketballs back and forth in the outdoors court by the gym. Eyeglassed bookworms, raven-haired young women, some with skin gingerbread-brown, others — Japanese, Vietnamese, the strengthening color of delicate rice powder — pored over their texts on the landing near the English and history wing.

A little late for school, Meggie dashed up the history building steps, Redwood shagging along behind her.

"Stay," she admonished Redwood at the propped-open classroom door.

The once blonde Miss Blount preened as she adjusted her eyeglasses on her head. "Today, class, we will discuss the Black History unit, starting with the first slave who arrived in Virginia."

Blount was always losing her spectacles.

Now Blount interrupted her lecture with, "Where are my glasses?" a question full of accusations, thinking as she did that one of the mischievous students had sneaked them off her desk and hidden them.

Meggie knew that at home Blount was the same way, for the teacher lived next door to Meggie, giving the girl ample opportunities to observe the woman's lapses of memory.

In class Meggie often wiped tears of laughter from her high cheeks, trying not to giggle out loud at the glasses sitting on top of Blount's head where she had pushed them and forgotten. Why didn't the woman just buy her some bifocals and be done with it?

Where were those tears of laughter now?

Today the laughter wouldn't come. Meggie only felt like tears.

Nobody told Blount the glasses were on top of her head. She'd find them. Eventually.

"So let us begin the unit on slavery," repeated Miss Blount with that smugness and sense of superiority people who see themselves as winners sometimes exuded like acne.

Meggie looked into her classmates' faces and all the students' eyes mirrored flustered frustration. The white ones reflecting guilt, the black ones shocked indignity.

Only Dennis Bell, who was once dropped on his head as a baby, smiled contentedly.

Meggie said from her seat in the back row, "I'm about ready to vomit. I'm definitely going to barf up

31

breakfast if I read another chapter about slavery and everybody I know my age is too."

The teacher looked at that mark in the middle of Meggie's forehead and the room temperature elevated. Stifling, felt like fireballs charging through the air. If you moved wrong one would hit you. Miss Blount wiped sweat from her brow.

Meggie, her bottom lip trembling, her midnight eyes fiery, was not thinking about Blount. Meggie wanted to go back and straighten out history. Rake a slave master over with his own chains. On the Middle Passage dump the ship captain in the bloody Atlantic and drown his evil white ass. Let the limbs descend from the trees and whip every lynch mob into the ground 'til nothing but their stubby heads was left.

"I want there to be so many prominent successful black folks nobody can be proud about being the first black congressman, the only black woman nationwide radio announcer. It's an insult, not a source of pride, to be sitting up bragging about being the first and only. It's all right to be the first, but it's a disgrace to be the only. Whoever's the only ought to be bringing more people into the light. First and only creates too many unnecessary jealousies between folks who ought to be working together anyway. I want there to be so many black stars in American skies you can't possibly count them all.

"When it becomes nothing special to be excellent, which we are, maybe a few more of us can lift up our heads and stop acting like we've forgotten our own yesteryears."

Students started sitting up straighter in their chairs and murmuring "That's right. Well?"

Miss Blount, when faced with this kind of unheard-of reality, tensely gripped the white chalk so hard it broke in two and fell to the floor.

Miss Blount said, not addressing Meggie's words, tension making her voice fragile enough to crack, "Meggie, why is that dog hovering in the doorway like a slobbering idiot? I told you not to bring that hound into this schoolhouse.

"Park that mutt outside!"

At the disrespectful reference to his pedigree, Redwood barked and raised the hairs on his shaggy back, then went dashing up to Miss Blount who jumped back, clutching her chalk to her chest.

"No, Redwood," said Meggie, calling the dog back. "You don't have to bite her. Something already took a chunk out of her brain.'"

Meggie swung out of her seat, walked over and knelt in the classroom door, patting Redwood.

"Those who do not know history are doomed to repeat it," said Miss Blount quoting one of the history book historians.

"They're doomed to repeat history whether they know it or not," said Meggie from the doorway.

Somebody said, "Yeah, we read about how these young black boys get roughed up and killed but maybe nobody cares because the same episode keeps on repeating itself. Just the other day I read in the newspaper — "

"I'm sick of slavery and I'm sick of things happening to us. I don't want to hear about anything else happening to black folks. We need to be responsible for what we do to each other today, not for what our forefathers and foremothers did or suffered. Whoever shot Billy Watson must have known

33

about those other injustices, but did that stop them? No."

"I know who done it," said Dennis Bell out of the blue; because he was a little deranged nobody ever paid Dennis Bell any mind.

"I saw. I know who done it," said Dennis Bell.

Might as well have been the wind talking, nobody even looked Dennis' way.

"Well, a lot happens to black people just because they're black," said Miss Blount.

"We were getting hurt back then and we're still being hurt today. And it's not because we're black. We've just been conditioned to think that's the reason."

Redwood barked an "Amen," as Meggie continued. "We need to look where we're going; looking back we often stumble and fall, can't see what's right there before us. Like what this present generation needs."

Blount looked from Meggie to Redwood then back to Meggie.

"What this present generation needs is more respect," Miss Blount clipped, white chalk all over her black skirt.

"For instance?" Meggie challenged.

"Like showing respect for the people who have to look at you. Appearances."

"Respect?" said Meggie. "I respect the goodness in people, no matter what their age or the color of the eyes looking at me. But I don't respect idle ignorance from any source. If the TV talks to me wrong, I turn it off. If I pick up a lying book, I lay it down."

"We can show respect by the little things we do. Take appearance," Blount continued.

Then Blount aimed her words at the class. "The

34

way *Nutmeg*, I mean Meg, goes around looking it's hard to tell the animals from the humans."

The classroom hushed. Miss Blount, who had one day overheard a student refer to Meggie as Nutmeg, because she sometimes acted nutty or different, had stepped over a dangerous line and didn't know it or didn't care.

Now Miss Blount swept her gaze over two of the Rastafarian-haired students and her voice became an ugly weapon.

By the way she wrinkled her mouth Meggie could tell she was thinking about a nest of snakes.

"*Nutmeg* lets the wind comb her hair. *Nutmeg* lets the sun iron her clothes!" Blount said, pacing up and down in front of the blackboard and summing up her point.

Sometimes the students couldn't believe the teachers' stupidity and some of them, tired of being taken for toads, dropped out.

Others grew film across their eyes and only saw what they needed to see. They buried these rejections and insults in a graveyard of their minds.

By the time they graduated they had entire cemeteries as underground, mummified cities, never to see the light of day.

"That's it!" angry Alton Gillespie shrieked. A freckle-faced boy with chestnut hair and cedar-green eyes, he didn't think he was able to stomach another sarcastic word from four-eyed Blount.

"How could you talk about Meggie like that?" he said, his voice incredulous.

"You know something," he said, getting up out of his seat, "it takes some respect to keep from cursing you out."

"Sit down, Alton!" Miss Blount commanded.

The whole class held its breath wondering if Alton would sit down and if he didn't what Blount would do.

Blount and Alton glared at each other. The fireballs just waiting for somebody to make a false move skipped up and down the aisles.

Then the bell rang. And the class let out a sigh of relief.

The outraged teacher, fuming audibly, looked down the roll book, stopped at "G" then scribbled a mark against Alton Gillespie in the ledger.

"Glad that class is over," said Alton as he joined up with Meggie and Redwood to walk to the chemistry lab.

"I don't know who's worse, Blount or Spellman."

"Boy, am I blessed," Meggie sighed, rolling her eyes up in her head, "and to think I live on the same block with both of them."

Alton and Meggie had the same chemistry professor, Mr. Spellman, who had been voted the most-hated teacher in the entire school. Spellman, an oily-voiced professor of cynicism.

"Can't stand the man," said Alton.

When they entered the classroom Spellman, skinny, skinny and the color of a brown rifle handle, was standing like a sergeant in front of a battlefield of desks with sinks and Bunsen burners.

A tension that had started in Blount's room continued building like an electrical storm you could not see, only smell, like the acrid fumes from a Bunsen burner.

An unseen cloud of sulfur hovered over the chemistry lab.

Experiment fifteen, the hardest assignment in the chemistry class so far, had been difficult for Meggie. But she had struggled with the problem until she chanced upon the right answer. She had meant to discuss the chemical reaction with Alton, but they had been so busy reacting to the wrath of teachers they had used up all the time between classes.

Now Spellman marched up and down the rows assessing each student's experiment. If the experiment was correct, he gave no praise but if it didn't look right, he mercilessly embarrassed the person.

Now, a stiff grin on his nasty lips, he stood rigid in front of Alton, shooting his mouth off like a shotgun.

"You don't have the equation right. You're not at home in your mama's kitchen making chocolate chip cookies, you know, where an extra pinch of sugar won't make a difference."

Then these sharp words shot their way out of his cabbage-breath mouth: "How's what you're doing going to turn out right, Dummy, if you've written the formula wrong?"

Spellman's tone of voice, picked up by every alert ear, sounded like a machine gun mowing down children yearning to learn.

Spellman snatched at Alton's paper so he could hold it up to ridicule in front of the entire class.

Before Meggie could catch her breath, Alton clobbered Spellman so hard the older man fell between the two aisles of Bunsen burners, his mouth jerking.

"For heaven's sake," said Meggie, going to Alton's side.

"You make me sick," Alton said coldly to Mr. Spellman.

Slowly Mr. Spellman collected himself up off the floor.

He pointed a finger at Alton and sputtered, "Boy, you're on your way to the penitentiary. You're trying to break into the jail house."

"At least it's not the cemetery," said Alton, " 'cause if I ever hear my name in your mouth again, Mister, you are on your way! They won't have to call the ambulance, they'll dial directly for the hearse!"

That very afternoon in the principal's office while Spellman was making sure Alton got suspended, Spellman developed voice problems.

"Pupil's name?" asked the principal, writing out the suspension order.

"G-G-G-Gillespie," Spellman gasped with difficulty.

A tightness around his vocal cords. It was as though all the teenagers Spellman had mistreated had their hands around his throat trying to choke the living breath out of him.

By the time school let out everybody knew Spellman had been whisked to the hospital where the doctor found signs that he'd never talk clearly again. He decided to resign that same day and to retire on disability.

On the way home Meggie and her classmates wondered aloud what had made Alton so angry, but when Meggie looked into their eyes, she could see the recognition. Alton had physically fought against what they all recognized but often couldn't articulate. The uglies.

Spellman gave you the uglies.

Three

Often Spellman, who lived directly across the street from Meggie, would get home from school long before she did, but today on her walk to Vine Street she saw him sitting in the American Savings and Loan building. No doubt seeing about investing his upcoming retirement check, she thought as she watched him through the immense plate glass window. Fidgeting in the heavy slat-backed bank chair, Spellman pointed to his useless throat and passed notes back and forth across the desk to the seated officer who serviced his account.

A teacher certainly can't pass notes back and forth to the students, thought Meggie. A teacher needed a voice, that's for sure.

"That Spellman sure loves money," Meggie said to Redwood.

She knew that greenbacks were a necessity in a world where money kept hunger away, kept a roof over her head. But the green she loved most was the green of trees, the green of grass and the green of bushes.

The color, the texture of green things filled up her thoughts as they journeyed home and before she knew it they were turning up her street.

Three elderly men, including Spellman, lived in the cobblestone building known as the Rhinehart house on Vine Street across from Meggie's place.

One of Spellman's housemates, a ferret-faced man, whose once mouse-colored hair had turned to silver, looked through the slatted dusty blinds at Meggie and Redwood as they arrived at her door.

He was *The* Mr. Rhinehart and his marbly eyes glinted and jumped as he watched the teenager and her dog.

Meggie's oaken front door led into a small Tudor, painted cinnamon-brown with copper-orange shutters. A cinnamon-bricked chimney looked like a hat on the edifice. The attic window glanced out on her front yard alive with September hues of dusty green: bay leaf bushes, Japanese bamboo, gardenia, cypress hedges and a cedar tree whose silversheen branches brushed the walls of the house.

Every plant needed a little water, every dusty garden waited thirsty for a late October rain.

An almost-green lawn, kept trimmed by Meggie, stretched out like a carpet around an emerald-colored pine tree.

Admiring Meggie's long legs and her irrepressible vigor, the old man said through a set of yellow false teeth, "Teenagers carry the fountain of youth everywhere they go," but he said this meanly. Since he had no grandchildren, he lacked the softening influence of grandfatherly love, an influence that sometimes moderates the reactions of the old when they consider the young.

Teenagers danced surefooted at the physical peak of life, Rhinehart thought resentfully.

"Such a robust and hearty girl," he said bitterly, sweetly, envy like venom in his voice.

Mr. Rhinehart rubbed his tobacco-stained hands together but carefully so he only gently touched the pain that blazed in his knobby, calcium-laced knuckles.

Meggie fished the key from her back jeans pocket and unlocked the black oak door.

As she and Redwood entered, filagrees of golden light from the oval stained glass set high up in the door spangled across her sweater like angel's hair.

Jehoshaphat dashed inside just before she let go the knob. The tortoiseshell cat was so happy to see Meggie and Redwood he danced fat-legged on the cocoa couch, the winged chair, scampered light-pawed from the standing brass floor lamp to the stereo left turned on to reggae music. Jehoshaphat danced almost in time to the reggae music showering them with notes from an acoustic guitar.

Meggie threw down her books and tried to dance too, rippling an air guitar, swaying her knees, dipping and locking. Her hips did not rock steady as a heart-beat though. Her timing was off. Redwood sat on the couch and just swung his tail and panted, too tired from fooling with People to move.

Meggie, if not in rhythm with the beat, did listen to the message of the Jamaican group singing, asking,

> Let's reach for tomorrow,
> Today's not all we got.

Turning off the radio and followed by her pets, she went into the bedroom.

41

Here was her special place. The lavender room enjoyed a southern exposure. To harvest the benefits of the southern sun, Meggie had hung crystals, water-drop shaped, in the three-paneled window. After-noon rainbows pierced the jewels just so.

Looking at the way light danced through them she remembered why early Indians called crystals the bones of the ancestors.

She kept one window panel open and it stayed that way, October rain or September shine. Today from this open space the natural incense of outdoor air drifted inside. The air, so full of the sun, smelled like the gardenia bush beneath her window.

In the corner on the avocado-green chair her ma-hogany guitar still waited.

But now she needed sleep more than she needed music.

She curled up on the bed, Redwood near her feet, Jehoshaphat resting in the crook of her arms.

She slept fitfully.

Thirty minutes later she woke up and stroked Fat, who looked as if he'd dreamed about catnip and girl kittens and butterfly-chasing. Surveying the chaos of bed covers, she thought she must have dreamed of monsters and ogres chasing her in a Billy Watson nightmare, her bed was so messed up.

Redwood perked up his ears as she picked up the guitar and pulled the strap around her neck.

Her fingers hunted for the right notes.

She played softly and surely. The melody rippled, dabbling in light and darkness, touching pain then leaving it to play a moment in a field of rainbows and raspberries.

She tried to play away all the sad moments of the

day. But inside her head strings of shotgun-thoughts ricocheted and her mind settled on teachers like Miss Blount who she suspected believed in history more than they recognized the present.

And history, she knew, was sometimes changed by whoever was writing it down, the victories transposed and justified to suit the wishes of whoever was in power.

But the present, it stared you in the eye.

Unblinking.

As unblinking and sometimes as ugly as somebody like Mr. Spellman.

She played on.

The Jehoshaphat cat watched a spider dangling from the ceiling, an eight-legged acrobat trampolining in time with the continuing guitar melody, one thread of sable sound.

The light from the crystal vibrated on the spider like neon.

When Meggie wove the last single plucked note, she heard the familiar jingle of her mother's keys.

Memory Alexander, tall as an Amazon, entered the house with a "Whew!"

She kicked off her schoolteacher shoes, flat and sensible Life Strides, and plopped down in the winged easy chair.

"What a day!"

Even though she was tired from the long soul-satisfying ordeal of the Panhellenic Council and the Sunday night return-home trip, she never missed a day of Monday morning teaching. When she saw Meggie she perked up. An even row of teeth earned her what Meggie called a million-dollar smile.

"And how was teaching today?"

"A hard row to hoe. Like plowing clods out of pasture. Jewels in the rough. Seventh graders. I have been slaying ignorance all day. Talking, talking, talking," she said, not meanly.

"How about some tea and biscuits?" Meggie asked.

"That's just what my mouth needs, something soothing enough to put words to rest."

Soon the room filled with the aroma of buttermilk bread and broomwheat tea crushed from the dried stalks and lemon-yellow flowers of the wild bush that grows in the red hills of eastern Oklahoma.

"How was Berkeley High?" Memory Alexander asked after sipping the tea down to about half a cup. The broomwheat gently muted her words.

"Awful," said Meggie. "First, Miss Blount called me out of my name. *Nutmeg*. Then Mr. Spellman made Alton Gillespie mad and Alton hit him and got expelled from school. Now they say Mr. Spellman's going to resign."

"Good riddance to bad rubbage," said Memory, looking out the window across the street at the Rhinehart house where Spellman lived.

"Oh, the state this old world is in. The problems, the problems." Memory Alexander frowned, little dimples deepened at the corners of her molasses mouth. A serious pug nose. Africa rich and lush-colored lived in the deep lines wrinkling her face. She continued, "Kids can't be kids for some folks lingering overlong in childhood. Old gray-headed fools in competition with adolescents. Eternally infantile.

"Just keep remembering what I tell you, Meggie. Some of these modern day Methuselahs don't have as much sense as God gave a goose. When it comes to relinquishing the things of youth to the young, they're like the dog sitting on top of the haystack, can't eat the hay and don't want the cow to get it.

"Everybody who picks up a book and stands in front of a class is not a teacher. Spellman's got a reputation among the teachers as being the kind of person who doesn't know how to look at young folks, just looked forward to collecting his check once a month. He looked at the check longer than he looked at his students, would look at a check long enough and could tell right away if a digit on his salary was off. But teenagers? Shoot. He looked right through teenagers, had already placed them on some low rung on the ladder in his mind. No indeed, everybody standing in front of a class is not a teacher. And as far as that nickname "Nutmeg" goes, it just means you've got spice. I always did have a preference for nutmeg, reminds me of your skin and your spirit. Spice-colored. Imagine rice pudding without nutmeg. Or sweet potato pie missing nutmeg? Talk about bland!"

"Even so," Meggie answered in a troubled voice remembering Miss Blount's meanness, "that's not what Miss Blount meant when she called me Nutmeg."

Redwood at her feet, as though remembering the tone of Blount's words, put in his two-cents worth of agreement. He gave a short bark.

Memory Alexander sat her teacup down and looked carefully at her daughter, a lanky girl who reminded her of a sturdy sunflower stalk, her legs were so long.

"Meggie, you mustn't be so intense about things. You know how teachers talk to each other. Blount is having technicolored conniptions. It's all over Berkeley Unified School District how you disturb the peace. When it comes to teachers you have to learn to take the helpful information they know and forget the rest. Daughter, drink the tea, leave the dregs."

Meggie was never good at apologizing. Didn't want to insult whatever bold spirit was causing her to be outspoken enough to uproot dumb contentment.

So she just gazed with affection at Memory Alexander, refreshed by the broomwheat brew. Her mother who had her own relentless temper often said, "Sorry is a sorry, sorry word."

That was the end of that lecture. Her mother was spreading butter and raspberry jam onto the fluffy biscuits and spreading a little more joy onto her life.

"I played my guitar today. Sometimes I wonder if I'm getting better or what."

"What did the music sound like?" asked her mother, going to the essence of the matter.

"Like a blue shawl of light," said Meggie.

"Well then, you're good, you are," her mother commented before yawning tiredly.

"Excuse me, Meg, but I must have my daily nap. These seventh graders have ripped the lining from my mind and only sleep will mend it."

Now Meggie alone in the living room replayed reggae words in her head while looking at the wavery light, fibrous as it slanted through the ribbed lamp shade.

She remembered the lyrics:

46

Let's reach for tomorrow,
Today's not all we got.

The light shining down from the old-fashioned floor lamp recreated a spellbinding pattern — a fragile, crystal lace.

Four

Meggie jogged while the just-risen sun lay sleepy in the sky. A morning haze floated like white autumn smoke through a canopy of moss-covered Douglas fir.

Eucalyptus Forest, two miles away from her house and farther up in the hills, filled a brand-new world with towering spruce and western red cedar.

Meggie's legs pumped, stretching to meet the earth trail, again and again.

Here birds twittered, winging through the pine-studded canyons, flitting through the sycamore stands and swooping down on honey locusts.

Below on the forest floor rough-scaled lizards scurried, rustling through the dead leaves and dry twigs, scampering out of the way of her flying feet.

Disturbed, even the rocks moved.

A girl squirrel hugged an oak tree branch then scrambled over to chatter on a limb as she watched Meggie race through the forest.

A spider scooted beneath a pinecone.

Mice skittered.

Meggie ran on, her lungs expanding, almost to a delicious bursting.

Sweat trickled down her brow and into her mouth. The saltiness fired her thirst.

Now she reached the young sequoia trees.

Passed the western hemlock.

Just fifteen minutes more of running. Almost time to turn around. Maybe when she reached the Sitka spruce by the curve she'd head for home and a tall cool glass of water before she died deliciously from dry throat and salt sweat in her mouth.

As she ran here in Eucalyptus Forest something began to clear up in her soul.

Something eased, undammed, sped with nimble speed to every needy nerve.

Something unlocked inside her head, shook off the biting chains, walked around freely in the upstairs of her mind.

Something rural, something rustic and untamed flowed primal as Eden before her eyes.

Art.

A poem of timothy grass pastures.

A painting of spruce low in the sky.

A three-dimensional photograph of sloping pines.

The first art that ever arranged itself in green blades and uplifted branches still here green centuries and green centuries upon the earth.

At last she rounded the bend where the spruce waited. She started to slow her loping gallop before circling back when she saw the vague shadowed shape of an animal sprawled on the trail near the canopy of black spruce.

"Why's that deer lying out 'cross the trail like that?"

Why would it sleep in such a vulnerable place anyway, a public path where people run and walk when there are so many tall trees and lovely meadows beyond the thickets. . . ?

"Maybe it's hurt," she decided.

As she jogged nearer she noticed the human legs, the back bent a little forward so she couldn't see the head.

"Oh it's not a deer at all. Somebody's tripped and fallen," she said to herself speeding up her gait, anxious to help.

As she shortened the distance between her and the accident victim, the haze thickened. Purple thistles stuck her in the scalp upsetting her newfound ease and crawling pinching down her back to her thighs.

When the stickers reached her knees she stopped before the reclining figure clad in a boy's blue jogging suit and red running sneakers.

She knelt.

"Hey!" she said.

He didn't answer. He wasn't moving. Probably passed out.

"Hey," she repeated, shaking him.

She pulled her hands back. The body was stiff.

She stepped over him to look into the face.

But there was no face.

Only a hideous wound gaping open out of the neck.

No head.

She swallowed hard.

No head.

She struggled between two needs. Finally she fought back her need to flee from Eucalyptus Forest and she gave in to her need to know.

Should have brought Redwood, one side of her

brain commented common-sensibly. But you like to be completely alone sometimes, the other side of her mind answered matter-of-factly.

She searched the brush. Looking, looking, also alert, peering anxiously over her shoulder now and then aware that the killer might be near.

Something about the size of a head lay in shadow under a bush of bitterberries.

She tiptoed closer, stopped and pushed aside the brush.

But it was just a large round rock.

A sigh of relief. A sigh of anxiety.

Better go back home. Too far away from the path. What if the killer. . . .

The trees whispered, "Look to the left."

Her body swiveled.

And there it was.

She stepped over to look at the clump of chestnut hair, then the ashen face. Shocked familiar cedar-green eyes stared pleadingly, vacantly at her.

She sucked in her breath. And the rocks cried out the name.

Alton!

It's Alton Gillespie.

Alton who'd stood up for her in class. Alton who'd walloped Mr. Spellman.

Dead?

Hiccup.

Dead.

She picked herself up and flew off the hill down through Eucalyptus Forest, hiccuping. Her jogging now turned into a race punctuated with hiccuping hysteria.

She ran past Eucalyptus Lake, past the mesquite,

past the scrubby shrubs, the white pine, the purple thistleweeds and the wild dandelion flowers. Still hiccuping. Scattering the crying rocks.

On out of the forest and through the waking hills she sped.

A driver, one hand on the wheel, sipped his first cup of coffee as his old sixties Volvo murmured and crept sluggishly through the morning. The driver watched half-surprised as Meggie outran his car, her chest heaving in hiccups. Meggie, Meggie, running, running down Euclid Avenue.

She did not stop until she reached Vine Street and her house, still hiccuping.

"Mama!" she screamed as she tumbled inside her door.

Her mother, startled from sleep, listened groggily to her daughter's raveled explanation. Meggie rambled, so upset about what she'd witnessed on the forest floor that Memory Alexander couldn't make head nor tails out of her words.

"Alton!" Meggie finally screamed so abruptly that the name loosed her throat, straightened out all the crooked words and now she screamed that she had found Alton . . . between screaming hiccups . . . dead.

"Alton? Who's Alton?" her mother asked as she crawled out of bed to call the law.

"You don't mean the Alton Gillespie you told me about yesterday?"

Meggie nodded.

First Billy Watson. Now Alton Gillespie. Why?

Lightning zipped through Meggie's throbbing head.

A corncrake hollered.

Five

A slump in her voice to match her downcast mood, Meggie talked to her dog the way she often talked to herself.

"Well, if I can't ever be alone again I don't know any better companion than you, Redwood," Meggie said, thinking about how she treasured perfect solitude and how unsafe the world was becoming.

"Is God sleeping? Where is this Master of ocean and earth and sky Reverend Marvella's always talking about? Up there slumbering in the sky probably. Head pillowed on a cloud. Snoring!

"We are being harvested," Meggie decided as she patted Redwood.

"First Billy, now Alton."

Up in Eucalyptus Forest blue jays, wrens and robins called warnings to each other in the temple of wind where evergreens watched.

Flicking their quick little wings, flying through arches of dust, hummingbirds looked over their shoulders even as they searched for nectar in the dry throats of fuchsia.

On a weather-worn bench shaped from experienced oak, Meggie and Redwood gazed out over the lake.

They watched the leaves floating on the water's surface, eucalyptus leaves jumping like green flat fish in movement that stirred and rippled the foliage.

A talking wind, dusty and dry, accented her sadness.

The trees bending over the water with the hair hanging down over their faces whined. And they were too tall to be the ghosts of Billy Watson or Alton Gillespie.

She shuddered.

But Redwood, scrunching down next to Meggie, thought he spied something delicious leaping at the edge of the lake.

While the dog was looking down, Meggie was looking up at the eucalyptus trees, through the green domes, imagining grandmother ghosts in gossamer gowns she could touch.

Suddenly Redwood sprang away from her as though a doggie bag of steak bones had suddenly appeared.

Watching Redwood darting between tall willows, Meggie soon realized that the steak and bones he chased was a wobbling toad hopping across the stones bordering the water.

Now Meggie followed the dog's progress, momentarily forgetting her sad concerns.

She was distracted by the hunter's look on Redwood's face as the toad bunched up its body, then bounced away to a lonely stone farther out in the lake just out of reach of his grasping paw.

When the toad took another leap, Redwood fell splashing into the water.

"Redwood!" Meggie called.

Redwood's unceremonious splash underscored

the forest sounds of insects. A screech owl disturbed in his hollow trunk hooted.

Redwood swam back to the shore, climbed up on the bank, then shook the water off his fur and with a disappointed look in his eye came over and lay now wet at Meggie's feet.

"That's okay, Redwood, I don't think toads taste very nice."

Now other voices reached out to them. But this time it was not the wind talking.

"Nutmeg, Nutmeg, Nutmeg!" a trio of boys with tiny earrings embedded in their left lobes chanted from behind a nearby family of birch trees.

Looking like mockingbirds, the boys skirted the path around the lake, darting and hooting.

When she got a good look at them she recognized them as the carpenter's sons. Muscular, like they had been sawing wood for weeks, they were the color of planed dark oak. The tallest one often sat in Blount's history class staring at her.

"Leave us alone, you striped skunk," Meggie ranted, glaring at the tallest boy.

"You old low-backed gopher!" she called the second one.

"Long-tailed, egg-faced weasel," she laid out the third.

Meggie said to the wet dog, "Who invited them? Let's get out of here, Redwood. See what mean people make you do, take the names of skunks, gophers and weasels in vain. I definitely prefer the company of skunks to these rascals."

But Redwood, taking a cue from Meggie's name-calling, snarled at the boys and started chasing them, barking.

"Here, boy," Meggie whistled in three short bursts that sent Redwood running to her.

"Nutmeg!" the three boys hollered again.

Meggie and Redwood started back down the hill for home.

"Nutmeg!"

The light in Meggie's midnight eyes ruffled the way light flashes on layered silk.

Then she stopped and without turning around gave the taunting boys a wiggle of her fingers in both holey pants pockets, eight fingers like spider legs abided perfect time with her swinging hips.

Six

Two weeks had passed since Meggie had discovered Alton Gillespie's body up in Eucalyptus Forest.

Nobody seemed to know any more than she knew the day she found him. The coroner's report still had not come out.

And everybody wondered who or what killed Alton.

In spite of her mother's warning to stay away from the forest Meggie still came, drawn and pulled by the bright and dark green foliage of the woods. In respect for Memory Alexander's concern and because of the fright the corpse had given her, Redwood always accompanied her.

Today Meggie sat on a bench facing the west. The Golden Gate Bridge waited for the fall rain to wash it more gold. Yet the bay view of the bridge was wondrously striking even with the few autumn clouds that framed it falsely promising a rain she knew would not come.

While Redwood roamed the trails, she hummed and played her guitar, rocking back and forth as she strummed.

Softly like the red sunset getting ready to fall under

the Golden Gate into the bay water and roll over to the other side of the earth she played.

Suddenly, between beats, she was aware of a presence behind her. And it didn't feel like Redwood. No panting. No patter of paws.

The air so pungent with the undisguised aroma of dry sagebrush coming from the mound of serpentine rock to her left had a slight musky sweatiness on top of it.

"Who?" Meggie wondered.

From afar she saw Redwood exploring the canyon below her. Bounding in and out of the mesquite shrubbery, he hunted the small creatures hidden there.

Definitely not Redwood.

She turned around slowly, thinking what a shame it would be if she had to hit somebody with her precious guitar.

She tensed, her fingers stiffly wrapped around the guitar neck.

Behind her she saw the tallest boy of the earringed trio who taunted her the last time she was at Inspiration Point. He loomed close enough to grab her.

Sneaky.

Her skin crawled when she realized how far from her side she had let Redwood roam and the sun getting ready to go down and the ghost of the head of Alton Gillespie still a memory on the retina of her eye.

"What're you doing sneaking around like that?" asked Meggie, her voice rising, hoping someone would hear.

"I'm not sneaking. I heard the music. I just — "

"You just come to call me some more names?"

she asked at the top of her lungs, scared but trying not to show it, so scared she forgot to give the three sharp whistles to her dog, but her loud voice did the job.

She saw Redwood had heard for he was racing toward them.

"Not today," said the tall boy.

"Oh, I see, you're by yourself. You're badder in numbers, that it?"

The staring boy was silent.

Redwood was on his way, running toward them, she talked louder.

"Thought you were the cat's meow. Come to find out you're the flea under his collar," Meggie ventured.

What if he's the murderer? What if he's the person who murdered Alton Gillespie?

"I'm not the cat, and I'm not his fleas either," said the tall boy. "My name's Matthew."

"And your co-hoppers?"

"I said we're not fleas. My co-hearts' names are Mark and Luke and they're my brothers."

Now Redwood raced on. Getting closer.

No, he didn't sound like a murderer. But murderers looked and acted like everybody else, often.

She remembered how terrible the boys' heckling had made her feel yesterday.

Fresh outrage stormed through her head strong enough to make her jaw crackle.

Redwood was almost there.

"Who do you think you're messing with?" she asked, her chest and chin stuck out.

She stood up, pushed the surprised boy back with a jab of her finger. "Can't you understand English?

Didn't I tell you to leave me alone yesterday?"

When she thought about Billy Watson and Alton Gillespie, how the innocent get picked on by the bullies, her playing hand knotted into a fist and she jumped up and, feet flying, kicked Matthew two or three times in the soft ache of his belly.

Caught off guard by this physical attack, Matthew stumbled back.

Stunned, the air knocked out of him, he tripped, falling.

Then he found his equilibrium.

His face screwed up, he lashed out, forgetting Meggie was a girl.

Matthew swung hard the way a carpenter swings a sludge he uses to demolish a wall in an old building he's renovating.

Power in his punch, his fist flew past Meggie's ducking head so brutally she could feel the wind. She wasn't quick enough though; the follow-up blow landed on her shoulder.

It hurt so much, she couldn't see the trees.

"God, I didn't mean to hit a girl," said Matthew in a shamed voice as he knelt to help her back up from where she'd fallen.

Redwood roared up and pounced on Matthew, growling, and his bare teeth went to work on the boy who was trying to cover himself with his arms to keep the dog from biting him.

"Sic him, boy," Meggie urged.

Teeth gnashing, Redwood wrestled Matthew deeper into the earth, washing him in the leaf-strewn dirt.

Redwood chewed through Matthew's pants, slashing his legs. Fraying threads flew and whirled with the dust, a mixture of stirred-up dried leaves and parched autumn earth. Redwood ripped the shirt off Matthew's back and bit the arm above the elbow that the boy used as a shield to protect his face.

"Call him off!" said the wounded Matthew.

Meggie sat nursing her shoulder. "Sic him, Redwood!"

"Call him off!" cried Matthew.

"Sic him!"

Then to the boy, "Don't you hurt my dog!"

"Hey, call him off!"

"Don't you touch a hair on his head," she warned the boy. "Kick his butt, Redwood."

"Call him off!"

The throbbing in her shoulder calmed a little. "Redwood! Sit!" Meggie ordered when she was sure the boy was bested.

Redwood reluctantly sat, but he kept his eye on Matthew.

"He's fierce," Matthew hissed.

"Protective," said Meggie. "It's all right, boy," she said to the dog, while glaring at Matthew.

Redwood growled deep in his throat because while Meggie said one thing, the tone of her voice said she was still upset with this boy.

And Redwood had mayhem in his growl.

"Hush now."

Matthew stood up and moved toward Meggie.

Redwood broke away from Meggie and leaped again.

For the throat.

Matthew dodged just in time.

"Redwood!" Meggie grabbed the leaping dog's collar and held him.

A swallow caroled and sound seemed to lose all dimensions. There was no top or bottom to the bird's call. And it flowed all the way to the bay and beyond that to the ocean without drowning.

The bird's pleading voice seemed to change the air around them.

"Listen, I'm not going to bother you," said Matthew. "I'm sorry about hitting you. You hit me first, and I was on automatic. A natural response."

Meggie grimaced, still stinging from Matthew's powerful left to her shoulder.

"I really didn't come out here to bother you. I just got a question for you, Nut . . . Meggie."

"I'm not the sphinx," said Meggie, on guard yet curious.

"Got some time?"

"That's all we've got," said Meggie. "Shoot."

"Meggie, why don't you like me?"

When Meggie looked at Matthew, she didn't know what she expected to see in his eyes. Under the thick lashes she saw a deep lake tinged with a despair she hadn't noticed before.

Spellbound by her gaze, he reached over and stroked Meggie's hand.

Redwood growled softly.

"It's all right," said Meggie softly to the dog.

Redwood tensed, ready to rip open Matthew's throat, but he obeyed Meggie's voice which now sounded easy and fear-free. Redwood leaned his head to the side looking at Matthew's hand stroking his mistress.

Meggie suspected that past the despairing eyes, down, down into the depths of this person was an inquiring soul searching for his own blue quality of light.

She pulled her hand away finally and instead of hugging Matthew which she was tempted to do, she plucked the guitar strings and stroked them into a haunting song of wondering that made Matthew think it was morning and bells were ringing in an empty church. And the song made Redwood settle into a mound at her feet and stay very still.

Meggie played remembering how Matthew always stared intently at her in history class. She saw that look again and what it meant hit her like a fragrant, cool breeze.

She blushed.

Her guitar strings became the loom she wove his question, "why don't you like me?" on.

She played until the answer echoed in the music.

The sun spread its last fire and winked its orange-golden eye before it fell to sleep in the San Francisco Bay.

In the new darkness she put her guitar down, looked over at Matthew and said, "I think I do like you. It's just that I was trying so hard not to be anybody's victim that I didn't notice you."

Matthew walked with Meggie and Redwood down the hill to Vine Street.

At her door beneath the golden light from the evening lantern above the porch, Matthew gave her hand a good-bye squeeze.

Then he turned away and walked down the hill.

Neither of them had noticed Rhinehart in the dark house across the street, peeking at them through his venetian blinds.

Seven

The three old men living in the Rhinehart house would remind any careful onlooker of the three monkeys that speak no evil, hear no evil, and see no evil.

One was croak-voiced and could not speak above a whisper.

One was almost deaf.

One was half-blind.

But all were evil.

The three of them represented something perhaps only a cautious realist knew. That the aged do not necessarily grow benevolent with the years.

A photographer taking their picture or an artist sketching their portrait might have mistakenly labeled them the good grandfather, the kindly old gentleman, and the wise elder.

In these three old men's eyes demons beat on strangely shaped drums, but one would have to have a particularly sensitive kind of metronome to feel the rampant rhythm of their evil.

The rhythm pulsated. *Tick. Tick. Tick.*

First off, they all rejected the signs of aging with pure unadulterated resentment. Another gray hair discovered after a fitful night of broken sleep could send Spellman, the retired teacher, whining into a whispering rage.

A slight figure, Spellman attacked his mirror. He held a strand of white hair in one hand and cursed out Father Time.

"Oh, you hump-backed, raggedy reaper!" he swore in a small wounded voice.

Tick. Tick. Tick.

The need for a stronger set of eyeglasses would set off Boone, a retired photographer, fuming, "I curse the light!"

And Boone lifted his fat feet, so fat they laid over his shoes, and ground the eyeglasses into fragmented shards.

Tick. Tick. Tick.

The innocent gift of a hearing aid was an indignity that sent a stream of spite spewing from Rhinehart's mouth. A retired first-chair violinist of the San Francisco Opera's orchestra, he roared:

"I used to love the symphony. Now I can't even hear it. And I'm supposed to be content with the *memory* of the sound. Well, I'm not. I definitely the hell am not." And he looked like he could strangle any silly bird that opened its beak to sing.

Tick. Tick. Tick.

They all hated to take their store-bought teeth out of their mouths at night.

They had no grace.

And they all lived together.

"Why, I remember," complained the half-deaf Rhinehart who had to always face the persons speaking so he could read their lips, "when I could hear carpenter ants chewing wood far away as Eucalyptus Forest my ears were so perfect." He folded his wrinkled lips over his false teeth. "I could hear an ant blink an eyelash! Could hear a rat piss on cotton!"

An ordinary person would never suspect the jealous venom Rhinehart harbored for the easy competence of young folk.

"Whoever said youth was wasted on the young never spoke a greater truth," Spellman added, all murmury and muffle-voiced.

Because all three men lived together they compounded their meanness.

Tick. Tick. Tick.

"I remember," said Blind Boone, purple veins protruding from his fat cheeks, giving a cartoon aspect to his great bulb of a nose, "better days."

Blind Boone continued, "I remember when I could see a flea hopping on a tourist down by Spenger's near the Berkeley pier all the way from my bay window high on Spruce Street."

"And I recall," said Spellman in that whispery voice, "when I addressed a crowd of students and parents in front of city hall after the great fire was busy burning down prizewinning buildings, I remember that the people could hear my advice all up in the hills. When I told them to hose down their houses to prevent the spread of flames, they did. Water everywhere. Articulate, that's what I was.

"And I think," he added. (His sandpaper skin revealed so many red speckles from overshaving on his scrawny face and neck that he looked like an adolescent old man with a fresh crop of pimples.) "I think" (His two companions had to lean in to hear his next words.) "that this heart of mine's about to give out. It weakens the weakest part of the body when the heart's weak. My voice. Your eyes, Boone, and your ears, Rhinehart."

"Now that we've found the perfect solution, I'm worried about how much it'll end up costing."

"What's money without health?" mumbled Spellman.

Boone nodded vigorously in agreement but stiffened all of a sudden. Alert.

"I hear her," said blind man, Boone.

Rhinehart rushed to the window. "I see her," said the near-deaf man after he inched two venetian blinds apart and witnessed Meggie watering her yard and talking to Redwood and Jehoshaphat.

"I can almost smell the blood pumping from her heart to her veins," said Rhinehart. "And I want what's hers."

"Got to do more than want," whispered Spellman. "We know just how stingy you can be with your pennies. A hoarder. It's a well-advertised fact you're sitting on top of hundreds of thousands. Probably own Wells Fargo, didn't you come out here with the horses?"

"Bank of America's where my money's at. Don't tell me what to do with my hard-earned cash, now!"

"Who's telling you? Hard-earned? You didn't work hard for it, somebody else did. All you did was invest it. No cause to get belligerent!"

"South Africa," Boone mocked.

"You can't stand powerless people either, so why're you worrying me about who suffers so I can be rich?" asked Rhinehart.

The men quieted then.

Finally Boone said, "When's he coming?"

"He'll be here directly," said Rhinehart.

"Patience then," said Boone.

"Time governs all," whispered Spellman.

"At least it used to," Rhinehart smirked.

"After this operation we can say we stole a march on old Father Time. Ha!"

In a dark nook under the ottoman trimmed in heavy silk, across from the couch where the impatient three men sat waiting, a spider watched. A black widow, shiny-oiled in her satin dress with a red hourglass just beneath her breast, was listening.

"Time governs all," one of them had said. Didn't she know it? the spider thought; she carried the time sign on her underbelly everywhere she went.

The spider, fascinated at the venom these men harbored, wondered where they mixed it. A venom more poisonous than even her bite. Maybe she could borrow a spoonful or two.

She folded her legs up under her, vowing patience. She wanted to see just how far they would go.

The doorbell jangled.

All three men jumped.

"I thought I heard somebody sneaking up," said the near-about blind one.

Rhinehart shuffled to the door and looked out the peephole.

"Well, well, well," he said, turning the knob.

The spider sprang up on her eight dark legs. She didn't mean to miss a thing.

There in the doorway just beneath the place where the spider's tarantula friend hung suspended stood a bifocaled man in casual attire, Hush Puppies on his feet, a medical bag jumping slightly in one hand, the other empty hand twitching, caught in a nervous movement that affects the sick and old. A patchy crop of gray hair straddled his head. When he operated, he had to take pills to keep his hands steady.

The gray-haired visitor sat down on the ottoman and proceeded to outline an amazing plan.

After a while the visitor left.

The black widow thought and thought about what she heard and saw; she couldn't believe her many eyes.

She wondered if the tarantula had been awake.

She had.

The tarantula hadn't missed a thing.

That night she sprang her scarred body up to the top bedroom and after about an hour of listening to Rhinehart snoring, the tarantula, feeling a shift in the atmosphere, leaned forward to hear Rhinehart's subconscious speaking through a dream.

"Charged your own mama interest. Then went on and ate a thousand black children's ears for dessert.

"I hope that money gives you nightmares.

"What do you think this is?

"Didn't you hear the drums in South Africa moaning and bleeding?

"Don't you know you can't dodge destruction?"

"No, how could I know that?"

"You know. Everybody knows that. You didn't care."

"I DID!"

"No you didn't. And you charged your own mama interest? A man like you, you're subject to do anything. You're gonna pay for that, oh yes you are. Africa, the mother of civilization, will not be damned. You're gonna pay!"

The light flashed on Rhinehart, a big bright illuminating arc of whiteness covered him like a sudden truth, and the sound was too clear, the meaning too insistent.

The spider saw Rhinehart jerk awake and let out a bloodcurdling scream. The spider saw how he still heard the echo of his own damned voice, and how he kept brushing the sound from across his face.

The tarantula rolled her eight mad eyes up in her head; she couldn't believe her ears.

Eight

It was sunrise when the porch spider at Meggie's house oversaw the unfurling of the tiny American flag at the top of the staff and crossed her legs satisfied at the way it fluttered red and blue colors dramatically from the front window.

The porch spider sent the word down the line. "Captain Alexander must be coming home. Memory has hoisted the Stars and Stripes!"

When the kitchen spider got the news she woke up immediately and started stirring around.

The kitchen spider liked to nest behind the warm corner pantry. Between the broom's straws she supervised the cooking of food, nodded her head when the concoction was right. She could tell the recipe cooks from the salt-pinching chefs, not by the aprons they wore but by the smells bubbling from their cast-iron skillets.

The kitchen spider was present when onions first got peeled and the vanilla tenders grated the vanilla beans and stirred the batter. When the coconut cake spoon got licked she was there.

The cheer in the house when Michael Alexander came home on leave from the army excited her. And she measured the pleasure of the welcome by the smile on Captain Alexander's face when he tasted his favorite meal: blackened catfish in Cajun sauce, string beans with red potatoes and red onions, hush puppies dipped in cilantro butter and washed down with ice-cold lemonade.

Sour cream pound cake with fresh-grated nutmeg was Meggie's own special contribution that never failed to get a blissful nod from her father.

On Captain Alexander's second day home, Meggie's friends increased the joy and noise in the house.

Matthew's brothers, Mark and Luke Davis, dated two sisters named April and May Spring. The Spring girls were known for their shiny black curly hair, one beauty more gorgeous than the other, with faces colored pineapple-golden.

April and May lived in the flatlands about thirty blocks from Meggie in a plain and simple rented house.

These girls' mother was always hollering at them. "With names like the ones I gave you, all light and springy, you'd think you'd be neater. But evidently you have an aversion to spring housecleaning!" said June Spring, she said this in spring, summer, winter and autumn.

June Spring had it hard trying to raise two girls alone. Divorced since they were nine and ten. And the effort was wearing on her.

When Mrs. Spring couldn't find beauty in the architecture of the house, she tried to arrange for beauty's presence in the interior by overindulging in order. But no matter how organized the rooms, no matter how spotless the floors, beauty wouldn't come.

"Sometimes I wish your father was still here," she would moan.

April and May's mother would sweep the girls right on out into the street with her harping.

She had created beauty by giving birth to these two tropical brown girls, but she didn't know that or had forgotten.

It had been more than two weeks since Matthew had startled Meggie up at Inspiration Point and asked her why didn't she like him.

For as long as Matthew and his brothers, Mark and Luke, were old enough to hold a hammer and a nail in their hands safely they had helped their father repair and build houses on the weekend. They didn't have as much time to date as they wanted, what with baseball practice and homework and carpentering. Because their father was a widower, they longed for the company of women. When they couldn't see April and May on their free time, they would stop by to chat with Meggie.

They lolled on the sofa, watched television, raked leaves, murdered the Alexanders' groceries, but mainly they talked to each other. Over and under reggae music.

It was not long after that that April and May joined the group that gathered at Meggie's. These girls whose mother couldn't stand their messiness were the first to pick up the stray popcorn and crushed Pepsi cans from the family-sized kitchen's tiled floors.

Especially after they heard Michael Alexander say his second day home from overseas, "Meggie, where'd you find these live models of womanhood?

We always did wish you had sisters."

All three girls rolled their eyes up in their heads as though they couldn't be more embarrassed, but they could not hide their pleased smiles.

Speaking of the carpenter's boys in a stage whisper Michael Alexander said to Meggie, "I'm glad you've got such intelligent friends, Daughter."

The boys were so bowled over they commenced to acting charming and like they always displayed the good sense they displayed when they were nailing two-by-fours and carpentering cabinets.

Two weeks later, the three shiny skulls of the cleanheaded boys started growing tiny whiskers that curled and shrunk the way black hair will.

"Buffalo cowboys," exclaimed Meggie, remembering that's what the Indians way back in another era called the black soldiers when they first looked at the Africanesque hair.

After a while the used-to-be cleanheads' profiles looked so acceptable that Miss Blount, Meggie's history teacher, and coincidentally Meggie's next-door neighbor, could look at them without turning her eyes away. In class she even called on the carpenter's boys and what surprised her even more was that when they raised their hands they knew the answers.

The trio of young men could now walk down the street without attracting snide comments from Blount.

This did not last long, however, for soon the hair got past the "neat" stage and when the three boys walked down the street with the girls, you couldn't tell the carpenter boys from Meggie, April, and May if you were walking behind them.

"It's a disgrace," Blount complained to Memory

Alexander over the exhausted telephone wires. "And I know you parents can't do anything with them."

And her fear increased.

The cleanheads had become longhairs.

"Longhairs. And I don't mean Beethoven," Blount quipped.

Now the longhair friends, male and female, called Meggie just before visiting her house, asking, "Old Stumbling Block, where is she?" Blount fit Meggie's definition of Stumbling Block. The Stumbling Blocks were people that Meggie called roadblockers; one put snakes in the road, one poisoned the wells of the spirit, one flagged down anything that tried to fly.

"What?"

"Stumbling Block. Is she at her post?"

"Wait . . . I'll check. . . . Yes, she's there all locked up with arthritis, perched on her piano stool by the window."

"What'll we do? Sneak around her or go straight in front of the witch's watch?"

"Give her wide berth," said Meggie. "That arthritis affects the temper."

"We got it, Buddy," answered Matthew.

This was the same day that Memory Alexander helped Blount weed her yard.

No two could have been more alike in appearance.

Well, almost.

Tall, both. A little plump, but pleasingly so. Wonderful wrinkles lined both faces. Wonderful dimples bejeweled both smiles. Both had crowns of silver hair. Their major difference was as small or as large as one wanted to make it, for Blount was white and Memory was black.

In attitude, however, there was a ravine as wide as Strawberry Canyon running between them.

"Now Blount, you have the prettiest yard on the block, simply because you fuss so," said Memory all clad in gardening gloves and a straw hat to keep away the autumn sun.

"Well, somebody has to keep up standards," Blount remarked. She wore a smart Panamanian gardening hat with a little fuchsia-colored ribbon around the band.

Just then a Mohawk-haired student came bopping down the street.

Memory saw him first.

She rose up off her knees and leaning on the fence exclaimed, "Just look at all the Art!"

"What?" asked Blount, looking at this outrage marching down her sidewalk. "Wouldn't be a bit surprised if he didn't smoke dope and kill old people going around looking like that. A purple-headed rooster!"

"Oh," said Memory Alexander. "The hair, the hair, the uneven purple of the spike hair. The asymmetrical and symmetrical way it sticks up and lays down. The way it clumps the color. Art!"

"Art? You call that Art? Senility is creeping up on you. Woman, have you seen your doctor lately?" asked Blount.

Memory Alexander was still staring at the youth as though she hadn't heard a word Blount said.

"You're just as bad as these rotten kids," Blount decided indignantly.

Just then a stray dog raised his flea-bitten leg over her lilacs and relieved himself.

"Well!" huffed Blount, taking off her gloves, signaling the end of the neighborly weeding endeavor.

"Guess you call that Art too!" she said wrinkling her nose at the dog puddle.

She left Memory Alexander standing there gazing down Vine Street, looking after the Art walking around with purple hair.

Memory Alexander said that night at dinner when Meggie complained about how the neighbors treated black male adolescents, "In all fairness to Blount, she feels she has a reason to narrow her eyes. She gets hysterical when she reads the crime reports in the *Oakland Tribune*."

"Then she gets further riled up watching the eleven o'clock news," her father added.

"Soon after the news she goes to sleep and takes that mess into her nightmares. What she saw some adolescent do to some senior citizen on Channel 5 becomes her own boogeyman when she falls asleep.

"When I was young, the boogeyman was always older.

"These days not so for the older folks. Now the boogeyman's barely stepped out of short pants. Not only that. Some folks like little black boys but are scared of black male adolescents, the way some people like kittens but can't stand cats, the way some prefer little puppies but can't abide dogs."

Meggie too had seen the eyes of some of the teachers looking at black boys, change from kindness and warmth in kindergarten to mistrust and doubt in the ninth grade.

Anybody unfortunate enough to let those icicle eyes rake over him shivered and got chilled right down through the bones. Left you with a frostbitten spirit.

The smart boy in kindergarten was perceived a troublemaker in the seventh grade. Same boy. Same energy.

"That's a shame," Meggie said out loud. "Must do something, something to you not to feel safe in your own neighborhood, in the place you call home."

She was remembering Billy Watson, roughed up and shot and killed.

"I'm trying to understand it," said Meggie. "But it's hard. I'm on the side of the kids. Something ought to be done and I'm not talking about Police Review Boards."

"It's a downright dirty shame," said Memory Alexander.

"Being on the kids' side?"

"No. That there has to be a side. We all win or we all lose, why can't folks understand that?"

"Because it's not true," said Michael Alexander. "In the real world, Meggie, somebody has to win, somebody has to lose."

She looked up at her father and a storm raged just behind his fiery eyes as he said, "Ugly people, may their tribe decrease. Ugly people will call you Nigger in front of your children while 'The Star-Spangled Banner's playing and the flag's draped over your coffin."

An uncomfortable silence fluttered, then settled an imaginary drop cloth over her father's face. Meggie held her breath. Memory Alexander started humming as she picked up a pile of students' papers to correct.

There it was, Meggie observed, just a glimpse of

it. That tenseness in her father, that same tenseness she had seen in so many black men.

The next morning Meggie woke up listening to the usual choir of birds chirping joyously up, up in the fig tree waving leaves outside her bedroom window.

She heard them before she could see them. A choir of birds threw back their heads and opened their feathery throats.

"Sounds kind of thin this morning, must be somebody missing in the choir," whispered Meggie.

"I forgot. I forgot to feed the cat," she said sitting straight up in bed.

She pushed her way through morning and to her robe and slippers.

"Must have been cobwebs in my mind. How could I forget to feed the cat?"

Down through the kitchen and out the back door she padded. She saw the birds crooning their tune, huddled together like a skinny-legged quartet and sure enough somebody was missing in the choir.

Below her, Jehoshaphat licked his lips. Choir feathers decorated the grass, such odd leaves.

"Meow!" sang Jehoshaphat, but he could not soprano like the puffed-up birds.

"I knew it. I knew it. Somebody's missing in the choir.

"I forgot to feed the cat," Meggie said over the breakfast table.

"That's funny. I thought you had," said her father. "He sure doesn't look hungry."

"That's because somebody's missing in the choir," said Meggie.

"What? What are you talking about?"

"Tell you later," said Meggie, a little disturbed. "School."

She thought as she made her way down Vine Street, why, in a world like this her father was right. The cat won. The bird lost.

Nine

While the singing birds welcomed morning, Redwood watched the grown spiders dancing in Meggie's October yard.

In the corner of the lawn near the lowest cedar
branch a mama spider instructed her children in the
fine art of parachuting.

Lined them up one by one.

Each tiny spider climbed up to the dizzy edge of
a cedar branch, faced the blue aqua sky and launched
forth, looping the loop, looping the silk ribbons that
the air played back and forth until the parachute took
each and every baby spider on a balloon ride.

Each spider giggled when it looped the loop and
flew away.

Redwood wanted Meggie to come out and play.

He wanted to fly away, like a circus of spiders.

He stood up on his hind legs and barked below
her bedroom window.

"All right, all right," she said, sticking her un-
combed head out of the window. Some mornings
Redwood was better than a clock or her mother's
voice or the choir of birds in the fig tree.

She pulled on her jeans and ran out to meet him.

Wagging his tail, he offered her his favorite stick from his mouth.

She took it and tossed.

He went dashing after, a streak of red wind, leaping across the red cedar bush and the jumping spiders. When he tired of chasing the stick and rolled on the grass under the Japanese bamboo, his eyes alert and his tail waving, his spirit reminded Meggie of the dawn of a red Sunday sunrise.

It was early.

Early enough to hear the "whack" of the morning *Chronicle* as it fell on the doorsteps and walkways of Vine Street.

Whack.

"Fetch it, Redwood," Meggie ordered.

And Redwood brought the paper into the house, bounding after Meggie as she opened the front door.

Michael Alexander found Meggie sitting at the kitchen table, her head bent at an intense angle, studying the front page of the newspaper.

The story said that a fifteen-year-old Berkeley High student named Donald Fuminori was found by the park rangers sprawled across the cowpath up in Eucalyptus Forest in the area known as Inspiration Point.

The circumstances surrounding his death were mysterious.

Fuminori, according to the reporter, left for his usual hike up the hillside on Saturday evening, near sundown, saying he was going to walk as far as the four-mile mark.

Later, his body was found.

Meggie said, "Listen to this, Dad. 'Anyone having information leading to the discovery of his murderer or murderers, please contact the Berkeley Police Department. Anyone who noticed anything suspicious around that hour in Eucalyptus Forest, also, please contact the Berkeley Police Department.'

"They didn't say how he died," said Meggie.

"That's because there's something unusual about the death," said Michael Alexander.

"What kind of unusual?"

"Sometimes there are ritualistic killings and the method has some strangeness about it."

"For instance?" Meggie prodded.

"Well, for instance," said Michael Alexander looking embarrassed — he hated talking about violence the way some parents hated discussing sex education with their children — "once someone was found murdered with her liver missing. Another time an eyeball was ripped from its socket and stuck in a victim's mouth."

"Awful!"

"Well, when those kinds of bizarre things happen the police keep the information secret so when glory seekers show up claiming to have committed the murder, they can distinguish the kooks from the real slayer. Only the real murderer could have described where the eyeball went."

Meggie shivered. "So cold to be such a clear morning."

Michael Alexander looked sympathetically at Meggie. Violence affected her the way it affected him and although he was a captain in the army where injury and death of soldiers was expected he never got used to encountering it.

The Alexanders' friends thought it odd that Meggie knew all about the birds and bees before she was seven. Sex was part of the cycle of life. Held an important place in the wheel.

Violence, though, led to death.

And that was another wheel altogether.

Meggie stared at the newspaper's picture of the scene of the crime.

There was a photograph of the gate, the gate off of Eucalyptus Forest, the one they all passed through to gain entry.

The light framing the picture looked eerie, as though the angel who kept day and night separated tripped and fell with the sands of time in her hands and thereby had gotten dusk and dawn all mixed up.

She looked closer. She had not noticed the tarweeds before, but there they were on the fringes of the picture, blooming too vigorously since summer had come and gone. What were these sticky smelly flowers doing raising their stinking heads proudly so late in the year instead of drooping, as was their nature in October?

It was truly odd.

What then made Fuminori's death so different that the police kept the details to themselves?

Out loud Meggie asked, "I wonder what happened?"

"I'm sure, whatever it was, it's enough to give us nightmares," said Michael Alexander who specialized in treating the nightmares of servicemen.

How could someone in the middle of autumn when the pungent mustards were dropping their yellow caps in the meadow, how could someone go out and murder somebody?

"Obviously it had to have been somebody who does not respect colors," Meggie said.

"Sounds like an interesting premise," said Memory Alexander who had just joined them to survey the Sunday headlines.

"What would make a person disrespect colors?"

"Lots of confused people in the world," said Michael Alexander.

"Just last week one of the servicemen said his mother-in-law was the kind of woman who sat with her back to the ocean."

"Anyway," said Meggie, "who could go up to Eucalyptus Forest and look at the wind poppies and think about killing somebody? Now, just who would do a thing like that?"

For a moment they were quiet, thinking about the wind poppies, their ephemeral petals fluttering when disturbed by the slightest breeze, poppies like soft orange butterflies dotting the gentle hills of the forest.

"Well, everything deserves to live," decided Memory Alexander.

"Even spiders?" asked Michael Alexander, an amused smile lighting up his dark face.

Meggie looked up; her father's voice teased her mother.

"Even the spiders," said Memory Alexander.

"When I married your mama," said Michael Alexander, "she couldn't stand anything that crept and very few things that crawled. The woman is a million times bigger than a spider, but many were the nights I've stayed awake killing mosquitoes off the walls. Now a snake, a snake will make her hurt herself."

"A snake used to, Dumpling, used to," said Memory.

"Remember that time you told your students they

could bring their pets to school, you were having show-and-tell?"

"Yes, I remember," said Memory Alexander blushing. "Seven-year-old Zachary Taylor came to class, hugging a garden snake just like it was a kitten.

"I tried to be blasé about it, but my feet wouldn't obey my head. While the children were petting the snake I was up on my chair and couldn't get down. All I could screech was, 'Get the principal!'"

"What did the kids do then?"

"Took their time. Got the principal, finally; they knew they'd treed the teacher in a chair. They had a gay old time, taking their time.

"'Course my fear of snakes was the talk of the school."

"The snakes might have been the talk of the school, but spiders is the family secret," said Michael Alexander. "It was a spider sent your mama into labor."

"What?" asked Meggie.

"A spider. First a spider scared her and she went into a dead screaming panic. Then she doubled over. I thought it was still the spider she was gasping about. Come to find out it was serious labor. It was you, Meggie, ready for the world.

"Memory, my mama says you marked the child."

"Well, if my panicking over spiders marked Meggie, she was indeed marked," agreed Memory.

"It's the two-legged animals you have to watch out for," said Michael Alexander. "And don't I know it! I see the results in my office on the base every day.

"What parents do to their children emotionally and physically is enough to turn you into a recluse.

"One father in the dead of winter had the utilities shut off because he was mad at the mama.

"Even what sisters and brothers do to each other can be devastating. One sister cut her baby brother's eyelashes off with a pair of sewing scissors because everybody admired his eyes. And there she was a raving beauty herself. A classic case of sibling rivalry."

"Beyond sibling rivalry which can be innocent enough, a lot of sickness in the world and all of it's not in broken bones and diseases of the body," Memory Alexander agreed.

"Lots of parents haven't grown up, and a lot of sisters and brothers hate the sight of each other."

"And strangers?" asked Meggie.

"Well, we've taught you about talking to strangers," said Memory Alexander.

"Strangers may feel freer to be even meaner. Kind of think that's what's going on in this case," Michael Alexander said, referring to the newspaper.

"I take that back about everything deserves to live. Whoever's doing this doesn't," said Memory Alexander, a hacksaw in her voice. "Better to stay away from Eucalyptus Forest."

Having said that she stood up and announced, "Time for my morning bath."

Memory Alexander thought about the fearless snake-loving students she had taught who'd gone on to high school as she soaked in the bubble bath, daydreaming.

But as she languished in the water, her thoughts turned from pleasant thoughts of American teenagers to dark visions of dank doorways and old men, toothless and mean, sitting before an early winter fire, trying to keep their bones warm and shooing old age away from the hearth.

Their rocking chairs parked in front of the fire

had wheels. And the men kept putting sticks in the spokes.

"Now, why would they do something like that?" she asked as she turned the faucet dial to hot to take the chill off the water.

Ten

Curiosity seekers went up to the forest.

They crashed the gate, clumping down the elegant clarkia plants, trampling the thirsty lavender petals and their dry scarlet throats.

Instead of running from trouble, they ran toward it.

Gangs of people looked at the spot marked in chalk where the fifteen-year-old Fuminori had lain.

And every one of these calamity collectors had a theory.

"Probably drug-related," said one amateur sleuth.

"Somebody had it in for him, all the signs of a revenge killing," someone else surmised.

"Oh, he did it to himself, you know we've had a rash of teen suicides lately," said an athletic-looking man.

These tourists of pain were scavengers of disaster trying to fill up their empty lives with other people's hurt, as though their own wasn't agonizing enough.

Inside themselves they grinned at other folks' graves, smacked their lips at the suffering of strangers. Got high off of grief.

An undercover policeman mingled with the

crowd, trying to pick out anybody who looked the least bit suspicious.

But what caught his sharp eye the most was a persistent hummingbird pollinating the ruby thistle.

And he didn't see anyone he wanted to take downtown in the wagon.

The carnival of fear left the people's voices and sat on the tree limbs that bent over Eucalyptus Lake.

But the spiders, now, the spiders were kinsfolk of fear, had seen its face so many times they were rarely surprised at anything humans did in the name of terror.

Some spiders up in the forest knew all about the murder.

They were astonished at the purpose behind it.

"Well, shut my mouth," said a tarantula.

When the spiders got to gossiping, one mother scorpion hid under a stump and kept her new babies busy so they couldn't overhear the horror.

The next week, seventeen-year-old Rita Gonzalez came up missing. The last time anybody had seen her she was heading up to the forest along about sunset.

Creepy and crawly notions burrowed under people's skin.

"It was just an unlucky coincidence," one reporter remarked on the nightly news, "that two teenagers met with bad fortune up in Eucalyptus Forest along about sunset."

Then the next week Regan Russell, the tow-headed star of the football team, a Yellow Jacket halfback, went jogging up Inspiration Mountain in the forest. And he disappeared.

By now the panic reached full scale.

Parents forbade their teenagers to go up there at all.

And the notices were posted up all over Berkeley, on University Avenue and Sacramento Street and on over to Ashby Avenue. Missing teenagers. Has anybody seen Regan Russell, six feet three, one hundred eighty-four pounds, a muscle man, missing, blond, a scar on his left cheek?

And has anybody seen Rita Gonzalez, a brunette, petite, a swimmer, able-bodied, but still a slight one-hundred-pound girl, perhaps unable to protect herself against someone using superior force?

But Regan, Regan Russell was nobody's pushover. Who would fool with him?

Rita Gonzalez and Regan Russell both last seen about sundown.

And up in Eucalyptus Forest the light wiggled and jumped from the bushes and crevices, up and down the trails it lit, it skipped over to the International Peace Grove and sat down on the monuments to Ralph Bunche, U Thant, and Pope Paul VI.

The light just couldn't be still.

Now it paused for breath.

Then it was off again running.

Eleven

Across the street in the Rhinehart yard, a steady stream trickled from a fountain and created a pond whose water was stained blue by the brightly colored rocks bedding the pond bottom.

On the ground in the shade of a weeping willow tree, whose sad limbs hung over the pond, bleeding hearts drooped among their fern leaves and bloomed odd flowers colored rose-purple.

The window above the pond was vacant.

No old men waited at the venetian blinds and watched, spying on the young girl across the street. It was dinnertime.

Inside the house in the living room under the ottoman the spider traced a golden eardrop in her web and listened attentively.

The three men sat at the dining room table, having a sumptuous dinner of fried chicken, mashed potatoes, peas, white Langendorf bread and Coors beer.

Boone, who had a love affair with food, looked with blurred dismay at Spellman, a finicky eater, picking at his peas, and chasing one around his plate with a fork, finally stabbing it as though it lived and he was killing it.

Today Spellman looked rather emaciated and as

skinny as a road lizard. His black skin was rough as a reptile. A bumpy Adam's apple bobbed an extra bobble every time he swallowed.

Rhinehart, sporting a tweed hunter's hat, ate moderately.

Of medium height, he used his entire body to converse, nodding his crop of white, white hair, tweeking his mop-handle mustache, and arching his thick brows which looked like white bushes protruding over a pair of deep set marble-gray eyes.

When he wanted to accent a point, he stamped his feet.

Rhinehart manipulated the conversation and ordered the food around in its assorted bowls and platters.

Boone gobbled a chicken heart. He forked great chunks of meat and pushed them in his mouth, barely chewing the morsels before swallowing. He looked like Santa Claus without his friendly red suit on. Or a Buddha without a Buddha's benevolence.

Rhinehart leaned back in his chair, stamped one foot and said in an extra-high voice, talking loud the way near-deaf people often do, "Well, we have a progress report from the doctor."

The two housemates opened their fish mouths in unison, like black and white twins of selfishness, greedy for what they didn't need and shouldn't have.

"What'd he say?"

"He said the first one didn't work because it was too long out of the body to do anything with. Had to get the timing down right."

"Well, did he?"

"Let me finish, would you? You'd think at your age you'd've learned some patience."

Boone stopped chewing for a moment, such was his vested interest in the answer. Very little came between him and his food.

Rhinehart washed a forkful of mashed potatoes down with a gulp of Coors beer.

He patted his mouth with an "R"-embroidered napkin. Then he took out his pipe and tapped the ashes out of its bowl before filling it with tobacco and lighting up.

Now he continued, the pipe hanging out of his mouth like a mouse tail. "Yes, he figured it out. The body's got to be kept alive until everything's ready. That's the best condition possible. No time between the body's parting and the parting of the heart."

"Sounds like a romance to me," said Boone, belching.

"The parting of the body and the parting of the heart."

"Except instead of being between a man and a woman or a boy and a girl, this romance's between the young and the old."

"A sharing of hearts!" Boone grinned just before wrapping his smacking lips back around a drumstick.

"How long, then, before we can share?" muttered Spellman.

"Doc said about a month."

"That long!" complained Boone.

"Is that long?" asked Rhinehart.

"It is when you're old and don't know if you'll wake up to see another day," whined Boone.

"Suppose you've got a point there," said Spellman whispering in that half-voice.

"What point? When you die, Boone, it won't be

from old age; you're digging your grave with a fork!" Rhinehart shouted.

Boone leaned over the mound of greasy bones piled high on his plate and reached for his bottle of Coors. "Can't the doc hurry this thing along?"

Spellman pointed in silent mockery to the chicken skeletons on Boone's plate.

Boone, who could barely see, noticed the blur that was Spellman's bony finger pointing.

"Just because you've got ulcers and have to sip cream out of a saucer and pick at your peas like a bird is no reason to attack me for my healthy appetite, Spellman."

"I don't think Doc likes us calling him every day, says it interferes with his train of thought," said Rhinehart, redirecting the focus back to their main concern.

"Anything that helps speed up the process is worth trying."

"Well, how long's it been since we took the money out of the bank? September. It was September. Could've been earning interest on that cash."

"Interest is based on time."

"Well?"

"If we don't make the heart exchange, you won't have much time anyway."

"And your money damn sure won't do you a nickel of good where you're going."

"They got plenty of rich men and bankers down there being barbecued in the everlasting fire," Boone cackled.

"And they'd pay a fortune for a cool drink of water."

"Or a six-pack of beer," said Boone, taking another large guzzle from the sweaty-cold Coors bottle.

"Water's cheaper. We're talking Profit!"

"Package it right, you can sell anything," said Spellman, paraphrasing P.T. Barnum. "Just look at the folks nowadays paying a fortune for bottled water. Water's damn near free!"

"I still say there's where you might make a bundle, if you could go down there and get back."

"Where?"

"Hell."

"Stop cursing," said Rhinehart. "This is a respectable house."

"Right, right, don't dishonor the 'dead wife's memory.'"

"Speaking of her memory," said Boone, "why are you wearing that hat at the table?"

"My memory of it is she wouldn't let me wear it at the table. Now I can, every time I call up that memory," Rhinehart answered.

"That money ought to be working for us," Spellman mumbled low.

"Life's the best interest you can get," repeated Rhinehart.

"Call the doctor one more time; how could it hurt?" said Boone, wiping the grease from around his mouth with a napkin no doubt left over from the deceased Mrs. Rhinehart's linen treasure chest.

"Who's going to be the one?"

"I'll do it," rasped Spellman. "I've got most of my money tied up in this thing. Anyway, Boone, you're too busy picking your teeth. Rhinehart, you called last time."

After he got up from the table Spellman went into the nearby hallway and dialed the number.

His two companions moved forward in their chairs.

"Good afternoon. This is Mr. Spellman. May I speak to the — "

Spellman's own throat choked him, closing around his larynx.

Rhinehart and Boone jumped up at the same time, like twin jack-in-the-boxes.

"Hand me that phone, with your no-talking self!" Rhinehart demanded. "How the hell's anybody gonna understand you bumbling and stumbling over words?"

"Look who's talking," Spellman whispered, his throat unclogging, "I may lose my voice from time to time, but you can hardly hear. Talk about the pot trying to call the skillet black!"

Still complaining in a voice Rhinehart couldn't hear, Spellman handed Rhinehart the phone.

Rhinehart continued in a clear, loud voice.

"I know I've reached the doctor's secretary," said Rhinehart.

"Speak up, woman!" Rhinehart said holding one hand over his unengaged ear and leaning into the phone. "I must speak to him. . . .

"Young lady, if you don't get the doctor to the phone I promise you I'll have your job.

"What?" said Rhinehart, his hearing fading.

Now Boone and Spellman were standing just behind Rhinehart, trying to understand every word said.

After what seemed like hours but was only a few

minutes, the doctor came to the phone.

Rhinehart's tone changed and tried to take on its usual equanimity.

"It's been more than a month since we first met. What are you doing, my good man?" asked Rhinehart.

"What? Talk louder. . . . We know it takes time. . . .

"Right. It is the only commodity we've got. . . .

"Are you threatening us. . . ?

"What? Louder please.

"No, we haven't changed our minds; why would you even ask a question like that? What?

"All right. All right. We did promise to wait until the end of the week. . . . What?

"Stop yelling!

"What? No, we haven't forgotten to stay on alert. . . .

"We packed the freezer, got enough food to last a year. No reason to go out except to empty the garbage. . . .

"What've you decided about the candidate we mentioned. . . ?

"What?

"Well, nothing like using a product that's home-grown. Right in our own front yards.

"Talk. . . .

"I know you'd rather not. But we know what we're looking at and this model has eaten right, exercised right and has a certain spirit that's rare.

"The heart of the matter, you understand, is this: She's one of the finest physical specimens this side of creation.

"We know you have to check her out.

"We know the plan calls for anonymity, but it's our money. And we want a say in the matter.

"No, we're not threatening you.

"We just want to live," Rhinehart said pitifully, his confidence evaporated just before hanging up.

"Wouldn't change his mind?" whispered Spellman.

"Nope," echoed Boone. "Nothing to do but wait a week."

Twelve

The KPFA morning radio announced, right after Meg-gie's guitar playing, that the Berkeley Police found the sixteen-year-old Regan Russell's body dumped on the roadside up in the forest.

The police were secretive again about the conditions surrounding the murder.

"I sure would like to be able to walk around in the world without fear. I'd like to take midnight walks if I want to," said Meggie to her parents who joined her when she took a music break and popped Jiffy-pop popcorn in the big stainless steel kettle then poured melted Berkeley Farms butter over the hot tender kernels.

"You've every right to be upset, but there's no way you're going to take a midnight walk out of this house and I know about it," said Michael Alexander, taking a handful of popcorn out of the heaping lacquered bowl.

"Over my dead sixty-three-year-old body," said Memory Alexander pouring three glasses of Welch's grape juice.

"A child rapist doesn't care one whit about your

rights," Michael Alexander informed his daughter. "Neither does the crazy man going around mutilating people. That's probably what the police are keeping to themselves. This derelict has mutilated some part of the human body and they're not staying which."

"Which part could it be?" wondered Meggie.

The next day when she met with her friends at Berkeley High Meggie repeated what her father had said, then added, "I don't like this curfew of terror."

"*You* don't? Imagine what it must be like in our house," said April. "If a plane passes over the house and casts its shadow, our mother screeches, 'Close the drapes, the madman's got wings!' At night it's hard to sleep, she's opening our bedroom door every thirty minutes to see if the Eucalyptus Murderer has snatched us away."

"Fall asleep finally, you dream about something terrible descending out of the sky and grabbing you. We're lucky to get to come to school in broad daylight," continued May.

"Well, I want to go back up to the forest. Up there where the air is free and the birds sing about it," said Meggie.

"What can we do about this madman?" asked April.

"Find this destroyer of the peace so we can get our forest back."

"But how?" asked May.

"Got to think like he thinks," Meggie decided.

"How would that be?" asked Matthew.

The six of them got quiet, trying to screw up their minds, trying to think like a madman, a rapist, a sadist, a person who enjoyed hurting somebody else, somebody who went around smiling when your house burned down, somebody who giggled when you broke your leg falling off a high limb.

Nothing came to mind.

"I don't know," said Meggie. "I kind of think we might be on the wrong path."

"What do you mean?" asked Matthew.

"Well, what if it's not a madman? I mean not a madman the way we think of a madman. When I think of a madman I think of somebody who acts without a motive. Something outside the person. What if this is somebody who's got a purpose?"

"What kind of purpose would that be?"

Meggie started to shrug.

Before her shoulders could come back down, a clammy hand gripped them.

She shivered.

Then the unseen hand with frostbitten fingers touched the members of the group, Matthew next, then one by one, the hailstone hands moved across all their shoulders 'til cold pellets rained down their backs.

April jumped and May hugged herself against the cold.

Matthew and the boys froze, still as statues.

Meggie started to say did you feel that? but didn't.

Each person thought that if they did not give voice to the chill palm of premonition, maybe it would disappear. So they just stood there, digging their toes in the earth, and saying nothing.

The bell rang. At the sound of its pealing, the chill dispersed, the silence broke.

"I think we'd better try to find out just what person

is responsible," said Meggie. "Anybody want to do otherwise?"

They might have said yes, let's forget it, a minute before. But when the cold hand of fear hacked them to the shoulder blades and left icicles in their marrow they knew they had no choice.

"Well, it happens up in Eucalyptus Forest, right around Inspiration Point. Why don't we go up there around sunset, all six of us, and see what we can see?"

"How're we going to do that without the folks finding out? We've got three families here."

Now they were walking back toward the school building entrance.

"And we're on curfew," said April. "Strictly forbidden to do anything but go to school and go straight home."

"Well, we'll have to arrange a meeting around sunset at . . . what time does your mother get home?" asked Meggie, turning to the Spring girls.

"About five on Monday through Thursday, but not until eight-thirty on Friday. That's the restaurant's busiest time."

"Why don't we meet at your place on Friday, and that's what the rest of us will tell our folks, then we'll hurry up to the forest and see what we can see."

"Hey, time to go, we'll be late for classes."

As they scattered, Meggie called out, "Anything's better than having a whole town of teenagers sitting like sitting ducks and scared to go to the places we want to go the most."

The six could hardly wait until Friday.

When Friday finally came, as agreed Meggie

dressed in army fatigues, khaki-colored in shades of green and brown.

"Why're you eating so fast, Meggie? Trying to get to the dessert in a hurry?" asked her mother.

"No, save the peach cobbler. Got a meeting at the Springs'."

"And how're you getting there? That's at least thirty blocks from here."

"Matthew," said Meggie, gulping her milk.

"We don't need to remind you, do we, about being careful?"

"Go ahead, join the crowd — the principal, the teachers, the police, other people's parents, the Springs' mother thinks the madman can fly through windows. Everybody reminds us that there's a hunting season for teenagers out there," Meggie answered angrily.

"I can see it's upsetting," said Michael Alexander. "Multiply that ten times and you'll know how we feel."

"You don't have to be careful where you go!" said Meg.

"I wish it *was* just grown folk having to be careful," said Memory Alexander, "I could handle that. I know ten ways to kill and others are hatching in my mind right now."

"Your mother was an Amazon in her other life," said Michael Alexander. "Hard to believe this is the same woman used to be scared of spiders."

Meggie's parents' concern made her choose and limit her next words most carefully.

They had some mysterious way of knowing when she was lying.

The doorbell rang.

"I think that's Matthew," Meggie said and sprang up from the table too quickly for them to analyze the words or the expression on her face.

She might not have bothered, they were too engrossed in their own terror for her, and so her lie slid her through the sticky web of parental fear and out the door into her front yard.

Thirteen

When Meggie thought about the parental web she imagined a web so vast it stunted mountains, made them look like pebbles, made the oldest redwood trees as incredibly small as blades of grass. And the web, the web it covered the world.

Matthew waited for Meggie out in the front yard.

There she walked into Matthew's embrace and closed her eyes. He hugged her so tight she could feel the tense power of his muscles right through his brown and green army fatigues.

Sighing deeply, she tilted her head up for a long, sweet kiss.

Then hand in hand they started out.

About an hour later all six of the fatigue-dressed, teen group crossed the gate and went into Eucalyptus Forest, winding their way up to Inspiration Point.

They huddled together, almost on each other's heels.

To the experienced eye they, in their camouflaged outfits, only looked a little like trees and bushes, mobile against the brown meadows and gentle green hills.

They spoke in hushes, already in their role as lookouts for lunatics.

"I think this spot's right," said Meggie, stopping near the path leading to the International Peace Grove.

Here, just off the hiking trail, the forest thickened with mesquite bushes and a copse of short pine.

"But the poison sumac?"

"Not so thick here if I remember correctly. But plenty of sow thistle."

It was five-thirty, one hour before sunset. The park was almost vacant. A few tenacious senior citizens out for their daily therapy walked the path, cane-free.

A little ahead of the older people, a teenager in a gray gym suit jogged along, looking behind him every few steps as though surely hearing again his parents' warnings about the dead teenagers up in Eucalyptus Forest.

He stumbled over little branches along the trail and finally he looked back so intently he slipped in a patch of cow chips.

May giggled.

The other five glared at her; they wanted to giggle too, but they dared not. Their eyes watered from the effort of holding in the laughter.

"What's that?" asked Meggie, listening intently.

"What?"

"Something. A roar."

"A mountain lion?" Matthew offered, trying to inject a little humor.

"No. Sounds like a motor."

"It's got a cough in it."

"No cars allowed up here."

"Look. It's a van. What have we here?"

They all leaned forward in the bushes. Six pairs of eyes.

Painstakingly and surely the yellow vehicle progressed.

The gears broke down and the van sounded as if it was going to stop.

"Oh," said Matthew in a dismissing tone, "it says 'Park Service.' For a minute there I thought something strange. . . ." And he poised one foot to step away from the bushes; it was time to go home anyway.

"Wait!" whispered Meggie, pulling him back into the cover of shrubbery. "Park Service isn't out here after five."

"That's right!" they whispered in unison.

"Why's that van here? It's not the plainclothes police; they wouldn't be in a van. They'd be mingling with the hikers and runners."

"Then who is it?"

"Maybe this is the clue we're looking for."

"You think so?"

"Can you see a face?"

Just as they all strained forward, the sun decided to take its swim in the Pacific Ocean. And it dived from out of sight, leaving a splash of darkness in its wake.

"No. Can't make out any features."

The van, swathed in darkness, stalked the awkward teenager who was determined to get his running in, Eucalyptus Monster or no.

But the teenager was wary. The cow chip accident had slowed his pace, eroded his confidence.

Over to the side of the trail he tried to scrape the mess off his sneakers.

When he looked over his shoulder and saw the ghostly truck in the new dark, he quickly joined the older people walking back down the path.

He fell in beside them, cow chip still glued to the soles of his shoes, and the van lost interest.

It turned its yellow self around and grumbled away from Eucalyptus Forest and down the hill towards civilized Berkeley.

"Wonder what that van was doing up here?"

"Up to no good," said Meggie. "This calls for another trip."

"Next Friday," said April.

"Now we'd better hurry," said May, looking at her watch.

"Takes an hour to get home. We've got to make time. Else Mama'll beat us home and park herself by our beds and we'll never get any sleep, sure as my name's May."

"Let's jog," said Meggie.

And they started running, like the deer who lived in the forest, but the deer bending over Eucalyptus Lake looked at the teenagers out of the corners of their velvet eyes and wondered at the young folks looking a little like trees and shrubs moving so resolutely down the hill, going into the town the deer visited more and more to get away from the evil that the lake had warned them about.

Fourteen

Thursday appeared bringing a mixed California cast of weather.

From her window Meggie watched the dance of lightning on Inspiration Mountain.

A configuration of white sticks clashing.

Far off a rumble smothered a smokeless smoky sky.

A white leap of lightning overhead. White hot to the eyes.

A long-legged acrobat strutted, hissing between sky and earth.

How lightning danced.

The hide-and-seek show changed everything to shadow; lightning, jealous of the light, left the red-leafed trees looking like a negative on a photograph.

The dancing line would not be orderly. It stretched every which way multiplying into more white sticks.

Magnifying in numbers, it zipped from cloud to cloud and talked back like a woman with her hands on her hips.

The threatening storm backed off. Then suddenly in patches the sun was trying to shine. At the same time thunder roared, lightning drew her long legs back up into a white cloud. A violent but quick earthquake shook the bedroom, causing the crystals in Meggie's window to jump and chatter against the pane, spiritual bones talking.

"Is that old devil beating his wife again?" Memory Alexander asked at breakfast.

"No, I think God must be knocking the devil in the head," said Meggie, the thunder sounded like a boxing match, and she imagined Satan hitting the canvas again and again.

As soon as Meggie pronounced this possibility the sky cleared and the sun stayed out.

That evening Meggie, head down, walked home from school late thinking about one of the lines in Reverend Marvella's last sermon: "The devil's only doing his duty. And his duty is evil."

She was trying to entwine this line into the murders. So engrossed was she in thinking about the devil and evil and Eucalyptus Forest that she almost missed seeing the envelope stuck crooked, lopsided in the mailbox.

Wonder why Mama and Daddy didn't bring in the mail.

But when she took the envelope out of the box she noticed the letter had no stamp. Her name was typed in slate-gray on its face, and there was no address under the inscription.

Who, Meggie wondered, her curiosity piqued, had personally delivered it?

A ghostly pair of frostbitten hands touched her shoulder.

She shivered.

Inside the house, she put down her books, opened the envelope and read the message from April.

Immediately she picked up the phone to call the

Spring house but nobody answered. Next she dialed Matthew's number.

"Matthew, can you stop over for a minute?"

She hung up the phone, her curious fingers turned the card this way and that way in her hand.

She jumped when the doorbell pierced her wondering thoughts.

"I'll get it!" Meggie hollered to her parents who were in the back of the house.

Matthew read the typed message out loud.

"Female teenager and her guest needed for a moonlight hike in Eucalyptus Forest. All other openings are presently filled.

"Your name was selected to fill the only vacancy.

"The group will meet at Inspiration Point at the mile-and-a-half mark on Thursday at 7:00 P.M. sharp."

At the bottom in the right corner was inscribed, "Police surveillance provided for your security."

"Thursday. That's today!"

"It's from April, with a little asterisk saying 'for girls only.'

"Females only, my eye!" said Matthew. "I'm going too. Always did want to be the only male around a bunch of women. Besides, a man might come in handy."

"It's comforting to see the police will be around, probably so many cops up there you can't move without falling over one of them," Meggie said matter-of-factly.

"It wouldn't hurt to give April a call anyway just to check," said Matthew.

"I tried. She's gone already."

She looked at the clock. "We've got to go if we want to make it there on time."

"Right."

"But wait," she hurried into her bedroom and shut up Redwood inside; they wouldn't need him for the group.

"Matthew and I are going to see the Springs!" she yelled to the back of the house.

"Fine, Meg," her father answered.

Meggie, taking Matthew's hand, was excited about the possibility of maybe discovering some more clues on this hiking adventure under the protection of the police and Matthew.

They started out. Here we go, just like undercover agents, Meggie thought to herself.

Fifteen

Up in Eucalyptus Forest at the mile-and-a-half mark, the full moon cast a crippled shadow over everything.

There was no April. No gang of hiking girls. And no police. A chill darted through Meggie's body.

The dense manzanita bushes nodded, urn-shaped blossoms bowed down in dust.

The crooked branches yielded brown fruit that sagged on the bush, almost dead from thirst.

The crash of the old oak tree on the lonely knoll a little distance from Meggie and Matthew sent a flock of sparrows chattering and fussing in flight from its toppling branches.

The thunderclap made Meggie and Matthew cover their ears.

Their nostrils flared at the reek of sulfur in the air.

Leaves, a blood-clotted hue in the autumn foliage of the white oak, trembled, still clinging to the tree's uprooted upside-down head.

Dizzy birds picked at the red berries of the fire thorns. The fruit from the pyracantha caused them to careen drunkenly until they heard a sound not too unlike the rumbling earthquake that troubled the oak tree.

The wind turned into thin black leather strips, whipped around and almost knocked the birds from the branches.

Both Meggie and Matthew turned to run, but mid-stride they stopped in their tracks. Before they could see it, they heard the van.

And then it was there.

Sixteen

"What do you want?" trembled Meggie when she saw the two burly men in the van stick their heads out the windows, rabbit teeth jutting down over their bottom lips.

Out of the corner of her eye she saw the nightmare wings of two vultures.

The vampire birds dug their talons into the scabby skin of the eucalyptus trees and hovered hunch-backed above the spot where the van stopped.

What did the vultures know?

"What do you want?" echoed Matthew, knowing often men didn't pay any attention to a woman's words, at least this type of men, he thought, sizing them up. If these buzzards bit you, they'd give you rabies, he guessed.

Bloodsucking bats knocked blindly against the hood of the van.

The two brutes with tobacco-stained teeth did not answer.

Twins.

They leaned out of the van, hairy apelike elbows jutting out of the window. Massive bodies of monstrous proportions, jaws like hogs, Meggie saw that much. Hands, calloused and cracked. Just looking at

116

them gave Meggie the gnawing urge to run and run and run and never stop.

The vapid faces in the van gave the boy and girl the once over, seeming to say these here are the ones we're looking for all right.

Their grimaces and grins suggested two horned devils who would grimace when most other people would grin and vice versa. Meggie imagined their looks mirrored the expressions you might see on folks who suffered from cankers festering on their inflamed brains.

One had a spasm in his face that twisted his grotesque features in such a way they shut the door on any thoughts of the man's humanity.

"What do you want?" repeated Meggie.

Still they did not answer.

The other twin growled raucously, sizing up Meggie.

Matthew's muscles popped up, bulging his shirtsleeves out. He'd kill if he had to.

My mama said she knows ten ways to kill, thought Meggie; I should have asked her to show me a few.

The two men descended from the truck and advanced.

One swaggering twin swung a tree stump, back and forth, effortlessly.

The one with a twitching face brandished a needle and leaned back against the van, patient.

Matthew swung at the man who wielded the tree stump, knocking him off balance, but the massive monster bounced back up as though only a mosquito had startled him.

Next Matthew pulled his leg back and with all his force lashed out kicking. His foot connected with all the brutality the evil-grinning men brought out in him.

The tree-stump-swinging man spoke not a word.

Then the tree stump swished up through the air and whacked down, almost pulverizing Matthew's flesh, in a language all its own, the articulate language of pain.

Meggie, barehanded, adrenaline pumping, tore into the attacker, her fist flying. She pummeled him, raining blows on his head, his neck, his back.

But he shrugged her off and she slammed to the ground.

Pain hiccuped.

Her ribs ached until she thought if she breathed she'd pass out. But the pain laid low it was so frightened and as she jumped back up, so did Matthew.

Matthew lunged first.

The ghastly pale assailant lifted the club again. Then the club, with a resounding *whack*, knocked Matthew out cold at Meggie's feet.

Meggie grabbed a rock off the trail, still hiccuping.

It flew from her hand as deftly as David's stone hurled at Goliath.

It hit the popped-out eye of her assailant and the man with the tree stump howled, clutching at the pain stabbing lightning from the socket to the back of his brain.

But the other twin who had been standing back whistling, waiting his turn, suddenly sprinted into action. He grabbed Meggie. And it was like trying to hold on to lightning.

All legs and movement.

She was too busy to scream.

Finally he wrestled her to the ground.

The ugly hypodermic needle punctured her trembling brown skin powdered with dirt.

And the goon grinned.

The twins tossed Meggie and Matthew's unconscious bodies in the back of the van and covered them with tarpaulin.

"The silent treatment carries its own terror, don't it?" said the twin nursing his eye.

"At least this time you was careful. Last time you used that tree stump you knocked that other one's head plumb off before we could get him away. Good thing the doc didn't know about that."

"Don't you tell."

"I ain't tellin'."

Next thing Meggie knew she was waking up surrounded by colorless white, cold white walls, stiff white sheets covering her body. She looked down at herself still clothed but wrapped in an antiseptic white hospital gown.

"We've been rescued," she said to herself. "The police finally got there. We're safe in a hospital."

Out loud she said, "But where?"

Nobody answered.

Wait a minute. There was no cord to call the nurse with. And why would she still have her clothes on?

Something was funny here.

All she could hear was the ticking of the clock.

She couldn't think.

Be calm.

How?

She imagined a blue shawl of warmth and the

sound of her mahogany guitar. Braiding strands of invisible light she picked the bronze string, playing the air guitar in her head.

The music tingled. Soft. Softer.

The clouds in her head started disappearing.

The blue shawl of light.

In a subdued voice the chords whispered.

She knew it was first light by the way the pale strands of sun reached through the window. By the way the sun's small fire played in the sky, it had to be just daybreak.

"Daybreak!" Her folks wouldn't even have missed her. They'd think she'd come in late and was still asleep.

She heard a low groan.

She moved her head painfully in the direction of the sound. Her head ached so piercingly it felt as though a rifleman was shooting, using her brain for target practice, reloading and backing up and starting all over again.

Matthew! That was Matthew in the bed across from her. He must have a headache too.

Now everything was becoming clearer. Of course he had a headache.

Those men, those men up in Eucalyptus Forest, those men up by Inspiration Point in the yellow van had slammed Matthew with a tree stump, picked up the weapon as though it were a toothpick and slammed Matthew on the side of the head.

She studied him. Matthew's head looked like a thousand yellow jackets had stung him. One of his eyes was closed and he groaned in pain even down in the false sleep the needle must have given him.

She jerked, trying to jump up and go to him.

Then she discovered she couldn't move.

She was buckled to the bed.

This was no ordinary hospital.

She opened her mouth to scream and then realized the advantage of being still and quiet, of pretending to be under the spell of the drug from the needle that had robbed her of consciousness yesterday evening.

She was glad she had locked Redwood in his room.

He would have ripped those rough men's throats open or died trying. If Redwood had mangled the men, she and Matthew would have missed this "hospital" connection to the murders. If the men had silenced Redwood she would have lost her faithful dog.

And they planned to kill her and Matthew, she realized. Like they killed the boy the police had found and wouldn't say what happened to him. Wouldn't reveal which part of his body was missing.

She gasped; she knew then what had happened to Alton; the one with the tree stump had knocked his head clean off.

Matthew was out of it. Too much pain, she could tell from the texture of the groans.

Her brain started working, slowly, like a machine that had rusted from nonuse.

I'm in a room, she thought, I'm in a bed in a room, I'm imprisoned in a bed in a room, I'm chained and imprisoned in a bed in a room. What to do beyond waiting to be killed?

"Meggie," Matthew groaned. "Oh, Meggie."

"I'm here," she said, turning her aching head with

effort. The headache was blinding. The hospital buzzing fluorescent light turned the pain a sickly green.

But Matthew's groans came from his deep false sleep. He didn't even hear her answer.

"Meggie," Matthew groaned. Matthew hadn't been kidding her then when he told her he dreamed about her every night.

Voices floated to her.

Not Matthew's this time; other voices. Not the horrid men's either.

As the voices drew nearer, she realized they were coming to this room. She shut her eyes tight, too tight, then made herself relax the lids so they looked more natural. Like natural sleep. But this sleep had been most unnatural, she remembered.

The two voices floated over her bed.

"Turns out the old men were right. Fine physical specimens we have here. That girl with the mark in the middle of her forehead is a real find. We'll make the change quickly."

"At what time?" the other voice asked.

"Well, we've got to get the old men over here. Prepped and ready."

"Can have them here inside an hour or so; they're home on alert waiting, they don't go any place."

The other person must have nodded. He said, "Two girls and one boy for three old men. Interesting combination. But these young organs, we've got to get them pumping, pounding at their height. Two ways to do that: exercise and fright. We'll use fright. That one over there with the bump on his head won't be exercising before it's time if we don't help him back to consciousness. Give him a shot, he ought to come around; then the fright testing can begin. Scare the heebie-jeebies out of them. Got to be careful though, too much for that last boy, he died of fright and his body part wasn't any good."

"That organ fairly stuttered. Couldn't use it after the donor died of fright. It wouldn't work right."

"You make me sick. Always repeating the words I've said. I'm the one with the master plan. I'm the one checking blood types and organ sizes by rifling the hospital records of these kids to match the old men's needs."

Meggie could almost hear the other one shrug.

Seventeen

Finally the doctor and his assistant left. And Meggie unglued her eyes and looked out the window. Judging from the strength of the sunbeams now it was about six-thirty in the morning.

"Matthew!" Meggie whispered.

She heard him stir. The shot they gave him was bringing him around.

"Meggie?" This time the voice was more clear, as though he was just groggy.

"Matthew, they've got us in a room. We're being held here for some kind of organ exchange for old people. They're going to frighten us almost to death and do it."

"Do what?" Matthew asked in a muddled tone.

"Matthew, get a grip on your mind!" she whispered fiercely.

"What, Meggie?"

"Matthew, we're in a . . . ," how could she describe where they were? ". . . in a hospital-prison, we were captured by two rough men last night, drugged with a shot, and brought here so this doctor could take one of our organs."

"Which organ?" said Matthew coming to life, and

thinking of the organ that all sixteen-year-old boys were shyly conscious of.

"Not that **one**," said Meggie quietly. "They want something I've got too. And I don't have one of those."

She wanted to giggle, but her fright scared the giggle away.

"Then what. . . ?" She could see Matthew try to pull himself up on one elbow and find out it was impossible.

"What the dickens?"

"Yeah," said Meggie in sympathy.

She wanted to tell him about the knot the size of a goose egg on his head but decided that wouldn't help matters.

"Meggie, I'll protect you," said Matthew in a stronger voice.

"We'll protect each other," she repeated as staunchly as she could.

Then she stiffened.

Voices outside the door.

"Here they come," she said.

Eighteen

The two rough-moving twins wheeled Matthew and Meggie, still strapped to their hospital beds, down a long winding corridor that seemed to continue forever through a series of swinging doors.

The farther they went the lower the temperature kept dipping. With clumsy precision the twins bumped their beds into the walls that tunneled them through the labyrinth.

Finally they came to the last white room.

Meggie's teeth chattered when the twins parked the bed.

The room here, chillier than the corridors, was as cold as January.

"Wanna bet on what scares these?" the twitchy-faced twin said to his brother.

The brother got all up in Matthew and Meggie's face. "Gonna be hard to predict just what these little niggers will git upset about. Never know about a nigger."

"Dunno, maybe the snakes. Worked on that other gal." Twitchy jerked his head toward the corner.

In the corner strapped in a bed just like Matthew and Meggie's a girl who fit the description of the missing Rita Gonzalez moaned. Terror had made a home in her dark eyes.

"I dunno. I dunno 'bout these here new pimple-faced patients."

"Let's see what happens with this little carpenter boy."

"I seen him before. That's right. Always helpin' his daddy so nice?"

"That's him."

They turned Matthew's head toward a screen. Images of snakes did not move him. Pictures of the tigers and wasps didn't take his breath away either. It was something totally commonplace and ordinary. Bees.

"Ayuh. We have it. It's bees. Who woulda thought? A Berkeley High Yellow Jacket scared of bees!"

"That'll be easy," said the doctor, entering.

"Now for the girl."

They showed the same writhing snakes, the angry bees and the threatening tigers. She watched, fascinated. When they showed her a family of crawling spiders, her face showed a higher degree of agitation and her pulse increased.

"I think we got it. Spiders," said one twin.

"Spiders."

"It figures. Girls don't like spiders. How do that nursery rhyme go? 'Little Miss Muffet sat on her tuffet eatin' her curds and whey, 'long came a spider and sat down beside her and frightened Miss Muffet away.'"

"Now that we got the instruments of terror, Miss Muffet, we be ready."

"Only a few hours before surgery," the doctor

decided. "Go get the trio of recipients," he directed the twins.

"Oh, Miss Muffet," said the one on the left, "I wish we could be here to see you on your tuffet, all frightened."

"Come on, quit looking at her like that. She done zung you in the eye once. I'm scared a her."

"She tied up, ain't you Miss Muffet?"

"Didn't I tell you to go get the recipients?" said the doctor. "Now scat!"

After the twin faces of evil left, the doctor stood writing in his chart.

Meggie thought she'd ask what the plan was.

"Why have you brought us here?" she asked.

"Curious?"

"Just thought I'd ask."

"Seems you're going to be part of a little experiment."

"What experiment?"

"Heart transplants."

"Heart?"

She could hear Matthew let out a sigh of relief, even though they both knew that without a heart the rest of the body parts you kept wouldn't matter.

"Why not do it the regular way, in a regular hospital, waiting for a donor to die?" asked Matthew.

"Oh, I've done that, but this is more experimental. You see, I have a theory. It has three parts to it. First of all, I believe a young heart at its prime is better than an older one that's been used too long or a younger one that's not quite developed. And so I chose to experiment with teenagers.

"Secondly, I think the time between death of the donor and the removal of the heart has to be minimized. In other words, the patient dies one minute and the heart is removed the next.

"Thirdly, I think the heart ought to be thoroughly exercised, primed, if you will, near the moment of death. It should be beating its strongest. Therefore we will instill fear in you until the heart is pumping quite rapidly."

"Oh, I see," said Meggie weakly as the doctor moved with his chart over to Matthew's bed.

Finally finished he turned and left the room.

"They tried with Regan Russell," said the girl still gripped in her vices of terror, her voice strained.

"Are you Rita Gonzalez?" asked Matthew.

"Yes."

"They're looking for you all over Berkeley."

She cried, "They'll never find me!"

Soon Rita's cry turned into a scream. The scream into a waking nightmare.

Nineteen

"I had this dream, this nightmare, rather," said Memory Alexander. A fragile glass shard of held-back hysteria chipped at her voice.

What Michael Alexander heard was this hysteria. Also, it was not Memory's words he was listening to so much as what she didn't say.

Dressed in his plaid pajamas, Michael Alexander hopped out of bed, pulled on his velvet red robe, then checked Meggie's room.

She wasn't there.

Because frequently she did not make her bed, he couldn't tell if it had been slept in or not, but Redwood whining on the floor tugging at the crazy-patch quilt with only Jehoshaphat under it did not make him feel more at ease.

If she had gone walking or running this morning she would have taken Redwood with her.

Then a cold certainty struck him.

This had something to do with the murdered teenagers. He rushed to the kitchen; last night's dinner had not been put away and Meggie's lemon-and-raspberry chiffon pie sat where Memory had left it on the table, untouched in its saucer from last evening.

Memory, scarlet-robed and wearing green high-heeled slippers, looked, fixed in one spot, out the living room window. She said, "The nightmare started with the yellow wildflowers growing in the Rhinehart yard. And then I saw this image of Meggie, but she wasn't there. 'Course Meggie's fine," said Memory, refusing to even look in Meggie's bedroom.

Redwood came into the living room and complained in that canine something's-wrong whine.

Memory peered across the street at the Rhinehart house.

Uh oh, thought Michael Alexander, she's out there on a limb of hysteria and sounding perfectly calm. And wearing those high-heeled slippers. A gift from one of her women friends. Something she would never ordinarily do, having once said "a woman should only wear high-heeled shoes as weapons."

"Why, it just can't be!" Memory exclaimed.

"What?" asked Michael Alexander.

"Those flowers over in the Rhinehart yard. Those flowers only bloom on rocky terrain, I tell you. Chaparral land."

"What's that? What flowers?" asked Michael Alexander.

"Thought I saw something shine on some golden eardrops across the street at the men's house."

Michael Alexander followed his wife's gaze.

"Something light over there all right."

When Michael Alexander looked at Memory he realized that subconsciously she knew that something was wrong with Meggie. She was trying to push it to another place in her mind where she could effectively deal with it.

And so she focused on the strange flowers in the Rhinehart yard.

"Golden eardrops definitely aren't supposed to have that silvery light. I'd better investigate," she said.

Memory walked across Vine Street, still in her robe, another thing she would never think about doing when her mind was clear, to get a closer look at the golden eardrops and to see what was making them shine so.

"Why," said Memory in the Rhinehart garden, "it's golden eardrops all right. So rare in these parts. And the silver is the silver of a spiderweb. What delicate tracery!"

Inside the Rhinehart house Spellman stood at the window looking out.

The telephone rang.

"What!? Yes, we're ready," said Rhinehart. "Five minutes!"

"Uh oh," whispered Spellman when he discovered the silver-haired Mrs. Alexander under the window. "We have company. We've been found out," he said in a squeaky half-voice etched with heightened alarm.

His whisper was so low and the excitement before them so fruitful nobody paid attention to Spellman. Boone and Rhinehart busied themselves putting on jackets, laughing at the prospect of stealing a march on time.

"Well, Boone, I think that plaid jacket suits you well, old boy," Rhinehart offered, generous in his hypocritical compliment of 'Balloon Boone,' the nickname he called the plump man in private.

At the window Spellman whispered, frozen in time.

While Mrs. Alexander stood in front of the Rhinehart house staring at the flowers, Michael Alexander took the opportunity to make some phone calls. First he called the Spring family and discovered from April that they all had gone up to Eucalyptus Forest last week in search of the killers and kidnappers of the teenagers.

"Wait," April said, frightened, "let me remember everything. We were supposed to go back tomorrow."

She listened to what Michael Alexander asked her, then answered.

"The only strange thing we saw last Friday was a yellow van.

"No, sir. It was inside of Inspiration Point where no motor vehicles are allowed.

"The strangest thing about it is this: It was after five. The Park Service wouldn't send a van up there then. And it seemed to be following this kid in a gray gym suit until he panicked and joined some older people taking their daily exercise."

Across the street Memory Alexander said, "I'd like to ask them how they got these golden eardrops to grow like this."

She rang the old men's doorbell.

Rhinehart said to the door, not seeing who was on the other side, "We're coming! We're coming! The van's here," he hollered to Spellman and Boone. "Going to get our hearts!"

Memory Alexander jumped at the rush in the old man's voice. So early in the morning —

Then she heard a roar behind her.

She saw a yellow flash.

"What's the Park Service van doing down here?" she asked the air.

Back across the street Michael Alexander looked out the window and his heart pounded. The van, that's the van April mentioned.

He called across the street to his wife.

"Memory, darling, we have a phone call!" And he succeeded in keeping the panic out of his own voice.

"Well, now," said Memory turning like a sleep-walker away from the door, "who can it be?"

When she got on their side of the street, Michael Alexander ordered, "Get in the car!"

Redwood dashed into the Volkswagen hatchback too.

"Why, Michael, the phone!" said Memory.

"The kids, the yellow van has taken them some-place and we're going to follow them. Meggie's not here. She's been taken someplace by these people."

Stealthily the Alexander Volkswagen backed out of the driveway and followed the van.

The three old men bounced in the yellow van's backseat, tipsy and lightheaded with expectation. They continued their joking in the speeding van for the duration of the short ride.

Spellman thought, I'm so happy, I'm hallucinating. When Rhinehart opened the front door, he thought, it was only the driver of the yellow van standing there waiting to whisk us away. And the Alexander woman he thought he had seen and that he feared had come to point her finger at them and keep them from their youth was nowhere to be seen.

All in my mind, he thought.

Twenty

"All in my mind," Meggie whispered. "This can't be happening."

Rita Gonzalez screamed.

She screamed until she didn't have much voice left.

Three glass cubicles took up most of the space in the entire hospital-prison room, except for an aisle at the end of all the cubicles and a small walkway between each cubicle.

Each of the three captives — Rita, Matthew, and Meggie — lay strapped to their beds in each cubicle. Rita was screaming third in the row. Matthew was listening to a low hum second in the row and Meggie was hiccuping first in the row.

The snake, evidently, had been hiding under Rita's bed. Now it unwrapped itself from the iron bedpost.

Matthew and Meggie wanted to cover their horrified ears while Rita Gonzalez screamed weakly, but they couldn't. Just as they couldn't turn their eyes away from the terror.

The snake now slithered coldly over Rita's neck then sat coiled atop her head.

And Rita screamed hoarsely.

Overhead in Matthew's cubicle a collection of

bumblebees buzzed madly in a round straw basket. The basket, hoisted high above his head, had a pulley of two strings hanging down from it.

Above Meggie another similar basket was hoisted but no sound emanated from her straw hamper.

Meggie whispered, "It's hard to think, Matthew."

"I know, but we've got to do something."

They saw the back of a nurse's head; she stood outside the door, listening before entering.

"Nurse! Nurse!" called Meggie.

The nurse, her cap peaked like a Ku Klux Klan woman's white dunce cap, looked in the window cut into the door. Her red eyes aglare as though she'd just come off a three-day drunk.

"Nurse, I've got to use the bathroom something horrible," Meggie hollered.

"Who cares?" said the nurse entering. "At seven-thirty you get the spiders. You're next, Sweetheart. I can't wait to hear you scream."

Meggie and Matthew both looked at the clock on the wall. It glowed 7:15.

"I'll make you a bet," said Meggie.

"A bet?" said the nurse.

Matthew groaned with dismay when the nurse turned sideways and he saw the pistol in the holster strapped around the waist of her uniform.

The nurse continued, "You're in no position to bargain, my pet."

"Still," Meggie tried, "how about it? If I don't scream, will you let me up to use the bathroom?"

The nurse's eyes smoked over, shifted, then she thought, what the hell? When they forgot to let the patients use the bathroom beforehand she was the one who had to clean them up before surgery so the doctor wouldn't smell the mess they made. Might as well save herself the trouble, but not screaming she knew was impossible, when she let the spiders down on this one, this one would scream as loud as the girl with the snake and she'd have plenty to clean up, if she hadn't already gone to the toilet.

Way she figured it, she didn't have anything to lose.

If the girl didn't scream, the nurse wouldn't have to clean her up.

If the girl did scream, which she would, nothing changed from the way it would have been if the girl didn't ask.

"Sure, why not? But I know you'll scream. You haven't seen spiders like the spiders we've got for you."

And the nurse, looking at the glint in Meggie's eyes, thought of terror.

The nurse laughed raucously as she looked at the clock and teased the girl, getting ready to release the crawling spiders.

"What have we here?" asked the nurse, jiggling the string holding the basket of spiders hoisted over Meggie's head.

"But first you have to unbuckle me," said Meggie. "If I don't scream, you're not going to come in here with these spiders and unbuckle me, are you?"

"Got that right, kid. I'm not coming into anybody's spider cage. Okay? I'm coming in there to unbuckle you now, but don't try anything smart. I got a pistol right here. And I know how to use it. Already used it, in fact, on that first black boy we got for one of the three old men — he got too violent. Had to kill him before the doctor was ready. Messed up the timing. Doctor couldn't use him."

"Billy Watson," Meggie gasped.

The nurse, paying what Meggie said no mind, went into the glass cage and carefully unbuckled the girl.

True to her promise Meggie did not move.

"That's a good girl," said the nurse, backing out of the glass room.

"Here we go," said the nurse.

Grabbing the string that she controlled outside the cage, the nurse slowly lowered the basket of three hundred tarantulas down from the ceiling.

The basket now sat on Meggie's belly.

"Now!" proclaimed the nurse.

She yanked another string and the straw hamper opened.

Three hundred tarantulas creeped out across the white sheets, crawled in and under the folds of white linen and onto Meggie.

"Ugly!" shivered the nurse as she watched the writhing mass, her face all screwed up, corners of her mouth turned down.

But the spiders smelled no fear.

Meggie started giggling.

"This one's gone mad," said the nurse, taking a Camel out of her pocket.

She tapped the cigarette with one long, red-speckled fingernail, lit it, then drew deeply on it as she watched the show.

The spiders swarmed all over the bed, touched Meggie, then explored the floor, the glass walls.

Soon Meggie stopped giggling when the spiders stopped tickling her.

And she called to the nurse.

"I'm coming out to go to the bathroom now."

The nurse almost swallowed her cigarette she was so amazed to watch the girl stand up. By now the spiders had left this donor alone.

Meggie walked to the glass door, opened it, and started to the bathroom.

The nurse took out her gun, "This one must be queer in the head," she said out loud, talking to the ceiling, but it wasn't the girl's head they needed and they needed the girl alive.

When Meggie passed the nurse she gave Matthew a conspiratorial look.

On cue Matthew started talking to the nurse, who held her gun pointed toward the bathroom.

"Do you like spiders, Nurse?"

"Can't stand them," she said in a perplexed voice, thinking about Meggie's reaction to the critters. "Why'd they leave her alone? Why didn't she scream?"

"Well, I'll tell you a secret," said Matthew.

"What's that?" said the nurse, all jumpy.

He started telling her about the spiders up in Eucalyptus Forest who had a People contest. The prize, said the king spider, would go to the person judged most scared stupid of spiders.

"When you're scared stupid you can't even scream," said Matthew.

This relaxed the nurse some and she turned around to face Matthew and to hear the rest of the story.

"Meggie turned out the winner," he said.

"How?" asked the nurse.

His story was so elaborate Rita Gonzalez almost

forgot about the snake, but she couldn't, she screamed in a chilly, raspy, almost inaudible voice. She went on screaming even when she saw Meggie creep out of the bathroom brandishing a heavy metal pole taken off an IV apparatus.

Meggie lifted the metal weapon and came down hard, whacking the nurse soundly upside the head, and the nurse slumped over and crumpled to the floor with her mouth open, her drooling spit sputtering out the ember of the Camel cigarette.

"Meggie, Meggie, you've done it!" said Matthew.

Rita wanted to cheer, but she managed to say, between screams, "I hear somebody coming!"

Meggie unbuckled Matthew and the two of them dragged the nurse under the bed.

Then Meggie and Matthew ran back into their glass cages and lay the buckles so they would appear locked.

Meggie screamed. She screamed as loud as she could.

The two-ton twins looked through the little glass window. "Yeah, it's working. One's screamed herself out, another one's screaming, Little Miss Muffet, and one screamer left to go. We're going to put bees down your pants, boy! Ha, ha, ha! Thirteen more minutes."

Then they were gone again.

Meggie and Matthew hopped out of their beds and released Rita, careful of the snake that had now slid back onto the bed railing and lay entwined there like the snake symbol of the medical profession.

Meggie took the nurse's weapon and she and Matthew put the nurse in the spider bed and buckled her down good.

Meggie and Matthew opened the window, then each took hold of Rita.

When they dropped to the ground the nurse came to and continued the sound of screaming.

She screeched in an ear-piercing voice, shriller and higher than Meggie's feigned hollering.

The spiders smelled fear this time. And they bit the nurse in her scalp, in her eyes, on her legs, got under her white uniform and bit her stomach, her hips, and one sat nibbling on her ear.

Twenty-One

The nurse's loud squalls still ringing in their ears, Meggie, Matthew, and Rita slid down the outside wall.

One of the first things they noticed was the yellow van parked under a warped-limbed elm.

There were so many crouching trees secluding the place that it was hard to tell just where they were.

The three crept low beneath the stiff-leaved loquat trees, smelling the white flowers of the tree, too sweet, the decay breath of death.

"Where are we?" asked Meggie.

"I don't know," said Matthew.

"Anything look familiar to you?" Meggie asked Rita.

"No," said Rita in her whisper.

"Did the snake. . . ?"

"It didn't bite me. It didn't bite me. All the time I was expecting it to, but it didn't."

"When we were taking you out of there I got a good look at it. It looked different. Come to think of it, I don't think it could've bitten you," said Meggie.

"Defanged," Matthew decided. "It couldn't bite."

"I already spent myself as though it could," said Rita.

"We know what you mean. It's all right," answered

Meggie as she gave Rita a pat on the shoulder.

Their surroundings looked familiar, yet unfamiliar. And the ride from Eucalyptus Forest had not been but a few minutes. Ten minutes at the most. Five miles from Eucalyptus maybe.

Meggie's and Matthew's muscles were so well-toned, they could run ten miles. But what about Rita? She wasn't up to much.

"Where the heck are we?" asked Meggie again.

"We'd better hurry up. Just go, no matter what direction. First we'll climb the fence," she decided.

A high wrought-iron black rusty fence peaked in sharp angry stakes. In places they could see a thin wire twining its way around the metal barrier.

"Uh oh," said Matthew. "Electrical wires."

"We'd be fried to a frizzle from here to Fresno if we even touched that fence."

Rita sagged as though she couldn't take another step. All spent up.

"Don't worry, don't panic," said Meggie, trying to think.

A sharp alarm disturbed the air.

Any moment the crew would be upon them.

The alarm sent them scurrying for cover between several scratchy, spiked yucca plants.

The whine escalated, then another sound joined it: fierce barking, the staccato language of a dog.

"Redwood!" said Meggie.

"Let's go!" said Matthew.

But Rita wouldn't budge. "I can't move," she said.

"Stay here. We'll come back," said Meggie, and they left the nurse's gun with Rita so she might protect herself.

Meggie and Matthew headed back to the center of their fear, back to the hospital-prison they'd just escaped.

Meggie stood on Matthew's shoulders and jacked up the window. She shimmied in first and he climbed after.

The nurse lay still sprawled in the bed and no one had rescued her from the spiders. She looked dead.

Cautiously they opened the door to the hallway.

Looked both ways, couldn't remember at first which way the twins had wheeled them in.

They started running toward the sound of Redwood's barking.

Running into dead ends where the barks echoed too faintly.

Turning, then running the other way.

Finally they heard voices and a more vocal Redwood.

"Why, whatever do you mean?" the doctor was saying.

"We think you have our children here," said Michael Alexander.

"Children? This is a geriatrics hospital!"

In the sitting room older people sat, the arthritic, the lame, the senile. Some with canes, others in wheelchairs.

"Why's that alarm ringing?" asked Memory Alexander, dangerous anger that she had pent up inside getting ready to cut loose.

"What's going on here?" she demanded.

Michael Alexander gave the room the army stare, fixing everything in its place, aware of everything that moved. He spotted Spellman. Rhinehart, ahead of him, was trying to sneak out the door, leading Spellman and Boone away.

"Spellman!" Michael Alexander commanded.

Redwood whined and scratched at the door leading from the sitting room.

Memory Alexander followed the dog, Michael Alexander followed his wife, letting the two men go in favor of protecting his very own.

"Don't open that door!" shouted the doctor.

"I think I'd better," said Memory huffily.

And she slammed the door open so hard the knob knocked the doctor down.

She brought her high-heeled slipper down on his hand as she rushed to meet Meggie and Matthew flying down the corridor.

"Call the law. They're killing kids in here," shouted Meggie.

"They're stealing hearts!" exclaimed Matthew.

"Whoever heard of anything so ridiculous?" said the doctor, nursing his hand.

"They've been murdering teenagers in here!" said Meggie.

Relieved to see Meggie and Matthew safe, already Michael Alexander had picked up the phone and dialed 911.

"People've been murdered. . . . I don't know where we are, this place doesn't seem to have an address. But I'm keeping the line open until you get here. Just follow the telephone signal."

Now the two strong-arm twins appeared, flexing their muscles.

"Those are the men who kidnapped us and hurt us, Daddy," Meggie accused with a pointing finger.

Captain Michael Alexander moved quiet and deadly.

He grabbed one twin and bumped his thick head against the wall, knocking him cold.

Meggie and her mother tripped the doctor midstride as he ran toward the door.

"That'll teach you to mess with people's children!" said Memory as she kicked the doctor in the groin with those high-heeled slippers.

Matthew punched the second twin and drew back to wallop him again just as the goon snatched Meggie back, eliminating the chance of Matthew getting in another hit.

The goon said, "Hold it, Mack, I got your girl. I'll bash her brains open."

At the same time the doctor jumped up and grabbed Memory just as the captain came to help his wife.

Memory's heart raced as the doctor pressed a scalpel to her throat telling Michael Alexander, "Come any closer and I'll use it."

Matthew and Michael were as helpless as babes when they realized the danger that Meggie and Memory faced. They had no control over what would happen next.

Then suddenly out of the tense silence, the scream of ten police cars whining around the corner unnerved the doctor and the goon, and they decided to get away before the police arrived. The cowards didn't get through the door before Matthew and Michael collared them.

Tension released, Meggie breathed easier when the officers walked through the entrance.

And even Memory, whose heart had been racing

faster and faster, managed to breathe a sigh of relief.

Meggie and Matthew led two officers around the side of the building to rescue Rita, the missing teenager, crouched between the yucca plants, clutching the gun.

"Rita, it's us. Rita."

Rita told her story, then fainted.

"Call for an ambulance," one officer told the other.

Next the police saw the room of glass cubicles, the dead nurse, the snake, the spiders and the swarming basket of bees.

"Whew!" said the officer in charge. "They weren't playing at all."

When Meggie began to explain who the hearts were for, the officer said, "Well, it will all come under investigation. Of course we can't accuse the patients of any wrongdoings, but the doctor and his staff will be arrested right this minute."

The ambulance finally came for Rita. It took her to Herrick, a real hospital, for treatment and observation.

Meggie and Matthew climbed into the backseat of the Volkswagen, with Redwood between them.

When they pulled up to the Alexander house, a welcoming committee of April, May, Mark, and Luke greeted them from the front steps.

"We got our forest back. We got back the Eucalyptus Forest," Meggie announced triumphantly, giving the victory sign with Matthew.

Too worn out to celebrate, Meggie announced, "Let's meet tomorrow. I'm going straight to bed."

Epilogue

Meggie went straight to bed and dreamed she walked around unencumbered up in the forest, that she played her guitar 'til the spiders crawled from under their stumps, unstrung their calligraphy webs hanging between the bushes and crept out of their tangled tracery under the pine trees.

When they were all assembled they swayed in six-eight rhythm, rolling six of their eight eyes and stomping their eight feet, until she set the guitar aside.

Then she stood between two pine trees.

Between one dedicated to U Thant and the other to Ralph Bunche. The spiders gathered in a circle around her.

"Confronted with so much evil in that hospital I didn't think I'd ever be warm again," she said to the congregation of spiders.

Glaciers in her breath.

She shivered.

Noon.

"Keep a light in your heart," Reverend Marvella had repeated in a recent sermon.

Noon. High light.

When Meggie thought of what God's forest meant to her, she thought of cedar, for cedar means the promise of life.

She placed cedar twigs around the circle.

Meggie braided cedar into her thick-locked hair.

Then taking her sharp-bladed axe she began to chop wood from the cedar.

She raised the axe and it fell on the wood, scoring it with a whack. *She broke the doctor of evil's neck. Sliced it in two.*

The sun warmed her and brought out the good sweat.

She raised the talking axe again. Armpits soaked with salt water. Sweat and splinters flew.

Spellman's wood flew out of the bark from the tree branch, looking like a neck with broken vocal chords.

She lifted the axe high and crashed it down again and again. *A woodknot looking like a cold Boone eye mocked her. She shattered it and sent a thousand broken eyes skipping along the forest floor.*

Rhinehart. Rhinehart, she cracked open ears, split them like eardrums with the loudest whacks she could manage.

The promise of life. A sprig of cedar.

Joy like the sap of cedar leaped up in her limbs.

She could see the noon light skipping through the trees.

The light in her heart. *Keep a light in your heart.*

Let not your heart be troubled; Meggie played the words in her head on an air guitar.

The noon sun helped her sweat away all the anger.

When her spirit was quenched she turned her face

toward the sun and chased away the shadows.

As the guitar song played in her head, Meggie made a covenant with herself.

She kneeled down and, bowing her head, prayed to God.

The blue shawl of light waited.

On the translucent cloth, seven crystals sparkled.

"Look closely at what the spindle spoke," a voice said.

She peered at the shawl. From every facet light winked.

And the joy made her eyes water.

"Put your hand on the crystal thread," the guitar melody called.

She touched a ray, a blue-purple iris stood up inside her.

The hate and the hurt fell away like scales.

The guitar sang every song it promised it would.

And the crowd of spiders looked on and waited.

Now she picked up the guitar, carefully placed the strap around her neck.

As she played the guitar the spiders responded. They moved with her down the hill, thousands and thousands of spiders following the sound of a mahogany guitar just blessed in the ceremony of cedar.

Without digressing she led them straight to the Rhinehart house and the guitar spoke its orders in rhapsody.

Meggie woke up hearing strange chord combinations juxtaposed on top and through each other. Eerie notes that together produced an unjangled sound.

A disturbed trouble made straight in the resolution of the melody.

She had slept 'til noon. She quickly dressed and reached for her guitar to recreate the sounds.

Cedar green sprigs. Cedar on the guitar.

The smell of cedar filled her room as she played, easily echoing the astonishing notes of her forest dream.

When she had the music just right, she looked up to see the familiar figure of Dennis Bell looking into the Rhinehart house and talking to himself. Loudly enough to hear him but not loud enough to distinguish one word from the other.

She opened the door and heard him say, "There they are. There they are. The ones that done it. . . . The ones that killed Billy Watson. Uh huh. Said they wanted a black heart. There they are. There they are. The ones that done it. . . ." Over and over again.

She crossed the street, wanting to know more.

When she stood by Dennis and looked in the window she saw the three men sprawled out on the living room floor.

At first she thought they were drunk but seeing not even a snore stir the mustache on Rhinehart's face, she ran home and called the station.

The police called the pest-control man and sure enough when he came to write his estimate he said that never in his life had he seen so many and so varied of the creatures under one roof. A web greeted him at the door, one brown scarred tarantula stood out from the rest.

Later on the pest-control man stopped by Meggie's to say that when the police got there they found a hoard of spiders had inundated the Rhinehart house.

"That's what happens in a house when a woman's not around," one commented.

The pest-control man said that surrounding the mother tarantula were many spider babies.

He found spiders nestled in the coves and corners of the ceilings. Black widows clung to the undersides of mattresses and under the ottoman and couches and chairs.

He had given a handsome estimate for the job he expected to do.

"Such tiny, tiny things. How could they have killed three men?" asked Meggie as she hugged the dog, patted the cat.

"The coroner said," boasted the pest-control man, glad to be the one spreading the news, "it looked like baby tarantulas and eggs were found inside the old fellows' brains, as though the spiders were looking for something soft. As though spiders had nested there and drove all three men insane just before they died from brain fever brought on by the infestation."

"Well," said Meggie, looking for a long minute at Redwood, "I don't believe a word of it. A spider wouldn't hurt a fly."

Redwood did not bark his usual "Amen."

He had been present sitting on a stump the noon of Meggie's dream.

Through the window Meggie watched the pest-control man drive off without accomplishing his mission because between the time he first saw them and when he returned to the Rhinehart house to spray his poisons he couldn't find spider one.

At last the first rain of the season started to fall.

Meggie watched a few drops of water turned to magenta rain, an illusion caused by a red light in the corner of the window.

In that corner of the glass panel a small baby tarantula with a lightning mark across her back tracked across Meggie's line of vision, then stopped and started weaving. Meggie leaned forward to get a closer look at it spreading a silver trail, remembering the last words she had heard in the green, green forest of her dream, a calligraphy made audible:

"When the people you ought to trust betray you, turn on the light in your heart. Nobody, nothing can keep you from it.

"If the unanointed preacher, the jackleg politician, the careless teacher, the abusive parent, if any or all of these should try to turn you from the light, tell them No.

"Pull the shawl warm 'round your shoulder. Keep your hand on the crystal thread. Tend long the steady, flickering light.

"Shimmer."

About the Author

JOYCE CAROL THOMAS received national critical attention when her first novel, *Marked by Fire,* won an American Book Award. She is a playwright and producer, as well as the author of five books of poetry and three other novels for young adults, *Bright Shadow, Water Girl,* and *The Golden Pasture.* She has been an assistant professor of English at California State University and visiting associate professor at Purdue University. Currently she writes full-time in Berkeley, California, where she lives.